DANGEROUS ELECTION

JOHN HEROLD

ISBN
978-1-963254-54-9 (Paperback)
978-1-963254-55-6 (eBook)

This novel is dedicated to Mary, my love, who has helped to keep me on track and in the groove, and to all the men and women in uniform who protect our freedoms.

The price men pay for indifference to public affairs is to be ruled by evil men.

— Plato, Greek philosopher, 427 - 347 B.C.

TABLE OF CONTENTS

CHAPTER ONE

"Arf. Arf!"

"Be quiet, Jaspar. Let me think."

Jaspar, an old English setter, was a faithful companion who loved to stay as close as he could to his master, the honorable Judge Leland E. Morris. He looked up to the judge much like a dutiful soldier, always watching his every move, always attentive to the judge's every need. Today, however, he sensed a difference in the judge's mood, and he didn't like it. The gray-haired judge, who had retired from his law practice six years ago, had found some personal happiness by spending most of his time in his little solarium, caring for his hybrid roses. Handling them with the loving tenderness of a grandfather, he had created the boldest and most beautiful striped crimson plants one could ever hope to see. Now their green stems were standing tall and their buds were beginning to reach their fullest bloom.

The judge had named them; "Red Harvest" because he was able to get them to produce in such abundance. Reaching his hands into the rich loam in the various flower boxes or occasionally relaxing in his moth-eaten recliner perusing a book on horticulture seemed to be the only joys left in his life. He ate very little but usually kept a stale sandwich in the desk drawer in the den.

It had been four years since the judge had lost his wife, Greta.

He had loved her deeply. Seven years ago when Rachel, their only child, went missing, Greta was overwhelmed with much grief and sadness. To compensate, she started her smoking habit again, which led to a fatal case of COPD. The judge remembered how Greta had fought so hard to conquer the disease, hoping to see Rachel's safe return home. The malady spread too quickly, though, and destroyed her lungs. Greta, simply, could no longer breathe.

This morning Jaspar could also sense the judge was grieving more than usual. With a missing daughter and no relatives to comfort him, the judge must have felt quite alone. Barney, the mailman, a longtime friend, would make it a point to stop by each day. He could see the judge was struggling, trying to carry a burden of loneliness and self-guilt on his shoulders. The mailman would offer him help, for instance, suggesting he should see a counselor, but the judge would always and very politely refuse. Grief was coupled with self-shame from a bad court decision; (he had set the wrong amount of bail in a murder case, thus allowing a murderer to escape). The judge could feel the weight of that mistake getting heavier and heavier by the day. Throughout his life of seventy-five years, the judge had always maintained a stoic fortitude and tenacious discipline that had guided him in coping with his family, society at large, and a few closely guarded secrets.

Now things were changing fast. An hour ago the judge, with the aid of a kerosene lantern, had reread the headlines in yesterday's newspaper and was well aware that a female cub reporter was digging up dirt, lots of it. She was delving into Mayfield's court history, which the judge did not like it one bit. He knew the townspeople were great gossipers, and he couldn't bear to see his family's name smeared across the front pages again. The judge felt he must act fast to settle all accounts and to put his mind at ease as well. He muttered aloud. "I am going to get that bastard if it's the last thing I do."

The early autumn morning was still carrying a sharp chill, and, for some reason, that chill seemed to have settled over the judge's small farm. The pull of the night was strong, but the sun was starting to gain strength, and little by little it was breaking the night's grip. The back of the judge's house was becoming visible. Dead weeds and fallen leaves lay strewn throughout a large meadow. A row of maple and oak trees guarded both sides of the open area. They had lost all their foliage and now stood as rugged silhouettes, like candles poking up out of a burnt pancake. The fast-flowing Whiskey Creek protected the far side of the meadow from any interlopers.

The judge, resting in his recliner, looked across the room and could see his backyard through a broken windowpane. He felt this autumn day was not one of nature's best displays.

Only the screech of a scrub jay somewhere in the distance broke the deadly silence. Then, as a few more streaks of sunlight began flickering through the row of trees, the judge knew it was time to set his plan in motion. He yanked the heating pad from behind his back, grabbed the car blanket off his lap, and threw both of them aside. He placed his hands on the arms of the recliner and attempted to push himself up to a standing position. His stiff body ached. Poor circulation, he assumed, as arthritic pains temporarily shot upward through both legs.

Finally, erect with just a little wobble, Judge Leland took a moment to survey the dingy walls of his home. It would be the last time. With the growing illumination that daylight provided, he could see the outlines of several household items. There was the flowery wallpaper he and his wife had put up when they had first moved in. Now it was stained and discolored by last spring's rainwater seeping through the leaky roof. He could see the crayon marks Rachel had made on the walls when she was three years old. Against his wife's objections, he had insisted that those marks not be erased. He noticed too that the sheet-rock walls were crumbling everywhere. A giant cobweb hung from one corner of the ceiling. The judge, though, seemed to care little. *Let all the creatures have their fun* , he mused to himself.

Then, for just a moment or two, he focused his attention on a large oil painting above the mantle. It was a portrait of his wife. He pined deeply. *Oh, how lovely she looked in her maroon velvet gown* , he thought. He remembered it was the gown she had sewn for his fancy retirement ball. On the floor he noticed the broken framed picture of his daughter, but he did not pay much attention to it. Instead he reached into his shirt pocket with his left hand, and pulled out a soiled handkerchief.

Jaspar barked.

It was the soiled handkerchief Jaspar had found yesterday evening while he was on his daily run around the farm. In one corner Judge Morris could see his daughter's initials, RAM (Rachel Ann Morris). He squeezed the handkerchief tightly, pressed it against his cheek, and started shaking. He was struggling, trying hard to get through a very emotional time. He tried with all his might to hold back his feelings. He kept telling himself it wasn't proper for a judge to have an emotional breakdown. His father, if he were alive, would not have allowed any Morris to show sadness.

Jaspar barked again.

Through watery eyes, the judge looked down at Jaspar. The judge knew that sitting there on his haunches was his best friend.

The judge managed to make a warm smile appear on his face, but it soon faded when he tried to reach down to pet Jaspar. The judge winced just once. "Fuckin' pain," he said under his breath.

This morning Jaspar knew something was really troubling the judge, more than ever before. By this time, he knew, the judge should have been in his solarium, digging into the soil, and planting new bulbs. Trying to pacify the judge, Jaspar ran over to the car blanket lying on the floor, took a firm bite, picked it up, and attempted to present it to the judge.

"No. No. Thank you, Jaspar. We won't be needing that blanket any longer. The sun is coming up fast. How 'bout we go for a long walk down through the trees. Maybe we'll see a bird or two along the way. You'd like that." The judge's voice was quite low and somber.

Jaspar became afraid, so he retreated, something he had never done before. "Come on, Jaspar!" the judge bellowed. The throbbing in his legs was starting to become more severe, and it was making the judge very upset. "The sun is coming up. We have to go *now!*"

Cowering with his belly touching the floor, Jaspar crept forward on all fours. He knew he must obey his master.

The judge, moving like robot, turned to face the wooden back door. His wobble was becoming less pronounced as he gained more of his inner strength. Three steps forward and his right hand grabbed the lock on the door. Unbolting it, he pushed so hard on the frame that the door flew open and hit the outside wall of the house, making a loud bang. Stepping outside onto the stoop, he heard the dry-rotted boards creak under his weight, but he paid no mind. A startled squirrel eating an acorn, looked up at both of them, and then scampered up the rainspout.

Acting like a good guard dog, Jaspar was staying close to the judge's side. Just once, however, he looked up and saw something unusual. There was a bulge in the judge's sweater pocket. A pearl handle was partly visible. Jaspar remembered what it was. It was the judge's .357 Magnum. It had been a gift from his wife, and he normally kept it locked in his desk drawer, the same drawer he kept his sandwiches in. Just once, a couple of years ago, the judge had to use the revolver to chase away a suspected thief trying to break in the back door. The loud noises from the fired rounds had scared Jaspar half to death and had left a lasting impression on him. Jaspar wondered just what the judge was doing with it, standing outside in the cold weather?

The judge winced as he tried hard to stand tall. He looked around, and sniffed the air just once. The coldness didn't seem to bother him. He took the revolver out of his pocket, raised it toward the rising sun, and spun the cylinder, which held only three rounds. He smiled. He knew he had all the ammunition he would ever need. "Jaspar, it's time we get that son-of-a-bitch; once and for all and find my daughter."

"Arf. Arf."

Next, he took the handkerchief that he still clenched in his left hand, and pressed it against the dog's nose. "Maybe while we are out walking you can show me where you found this handkerchief."

"Arf. Arf."

The judge did not put the revolver back in his pocket but held it close to his side, his fingers clutching it tightly. Together, the honorable Judge Leland Morris and his faithful companion, Jaspar, slowly started walking toward the trees and beyond. They had a date with destiny.

CHAPTER TWO

Lizzie Bateman, a retired veterinarian, liked to sleep late, and sometimes she would forget to check the coal furnace in the basement. She was a very, very sound sleeper and not even one of Thor's thunderclaps would wake her up, that is, unless it was happening directly overhead. But this night would prove to be quite different. For some unknown reason, through the depths of her slumber, she thought she heard three gunshots. They sounded very close together, and somewhere off in the distance, possibly near Whiskey Creek in back of the judge's farm.

Instantly, Lizzie froze and her mind became alert to all possible dangers. She remained quiet for a few minutes and listened. She was waiting to hear more gunshots, more sounds of any kind. But there was nothing but dead silence. And now that silence was making her recall the time years before when her husband had put a pistol to his head and pulled the trigger. She felt a growing eeriness inside her, and it was making her feel very much alone. All the fears of the unknown were racing through her brain. She began fretting and pondering what the sounds might mean. Was it a dream or nightmare? Were they really gunshots she heard? She knew it wasn't deer-hunting season. She even wondered if somebody might be hurt and lying in the fields behind her house? Being a very caring person, she felt she should be doing something. But what?

Lizzie tried to raise her eyelids. It was only a partial success. Mr. Sandman was allowing her eyes to become slits and nothing more. She could not see any objects, but she could detect, however, a few rays of daylight that were filtering through the worn window shade next to her bed. Her mind continued to race. *Maybe that stupid Alfa character that roams around here shot another wild hog*, she thought. Her father had always said it could take three shots to bring down an old tusker. Maybe that was it. Lizzie tried to roll her rotund body over on its side, wanting to stare at the illuminated numbers on the alarm clock. She prized that clock because it was a cherished birthday gift from her daughter, Samantha, and it kept perfect time.

She made one attempt at rolling over, but it was unsuccessful. She was determined to try harder. The second time she succeeded so well that she almost rolled off the bed. Lizzie looked up at the illumination and tried hard to make out the numbers. In desperation, she rubbed her eyes with her forefingers, and then grabbed the trifocals off the nightstand. With one steady hand, she held them close to her eyes, and she even craned her neck a little to get a closer look. The digital numbers seemed to read 6:23 a.m., but she still wasn't quite sure. Waiting a few seconds, Lizzie knew that the cobwebs in her brain would be fast disappearing, and that her eyesight would rapidly improve. She continued to focus on the pale blue color of each number.

Like magic, Mr. Sandman disappeared and her vision became crystal clear. The slits had given way to fully opened eyes. Yes, it was 6:23 a.m. She was sure of it. Lizzie thought for a moment. She had to make a decision. She was positive she had locked all the doors and windows the previous afternoon, right after the mail had been delivered, maybe 5:00 p.m. No one could possibly get inside. Her house was locked up tighter than a drum. Therefore, she reasoned, the house was secure and the sounds she might have heard were simply too far away to mean any harm might come to her. "Screw it," Lizzie muttered aloud. "It's too damn early to get up at this hour."

She placed the trifocals back on the nightstand, pulled the top edge of the blanket over her body, and plopped her head down. It hit something hard. Lizzie slid her hand out from under the pillows, and touched it. It was the novel she had been reading last night.

Annoyed even more, she grabbed it and threw it across the bed.

She fluffed up her two downy pillows in hopes of finding some more rest. Lizzie, being a strong-willed person, had made up her mind. She would go back to sleep and forget the whole damn thing. Period.

But as Lizzie snuggled her head within the pillows, she couldn't stop remembering something. She had observed her breath rising toward the ceiling. She also began to feel a growing chill and numbness in the lower parts of her body. With a quick glance over her shoulder, she realized what was wrong. When she had rolled over to check the time, she had pulled a corner of the blanket off her left leg.

"Damn it. Can't I get any sleep around here?" She mumbled. "Nobody needs to get up this early?"

Lizzie slid her left foot back under the blanket and rubbed it against her warm right calf. The left foot felt icy cold. The TV weatherman had said it was going to be a cold evening, and Lizzie now knew he was right in his prediction. *Probably thirty- five degrees in this damn house* , Lizzie thought, and she also knew exactly what was wrong. The fire in the furnace had to be almost out, probably because she had forgotten to set one of the dampers before going to bed.

She tossed the entire blanket aside and sat up on the edge of the bed, her legs barely touching the floor. She slid her feet into a pair of old slippers, and reached for the robe draped over the bedpost. With the sudden energy of a teenager, she scampered across the linoleum floor, through the kitchen, and over to the basement door where she flipped on the light switch. As she started down the stairs, one of her slippers became snagged on a step and she almost tumbled down the rest of them. But, by some miracle, Lizzie was able to keep her balance. She reached the concrete floor standing up. The first thing she detected was a stifling heat. Then she got a strong whiff of a rancid, and unpleasant odor permeating the entire area. Lizzie hurried to the far wall next to the coal bin, where the furnace stood. She noticed a thin trail of coal dust on the floor between the coal bin and the furnace door. It was something she would never allow, because she wouldn't want anybody to step on it and track it upstairs. It was a complete puzzle to her how it could have gotten there, but she decided she would clean it up later in the day.

Lizzie checked the dampers, one on the top door and one on the bottom door of the furnace. They were closed. Then she walked behind the furnace and grabbed the handle on the side of the heating duct. She tried turning it. Sure enough, she could tell the damper had been closed. Lizzie opened it halfway to allow any heat left in the furnace to reach the upstairs. Smell or no smell, she would have some heat.

Next, she checked the contents in the furnace. With the corner of her robe, she lifted the warm latch handle on the top door of the furnace and swung it open. Inside, the fire was just a little glow, but Lizzie could make out that some of the coals appeared not to be completely burned. She could see she would have to add more coal. Lizzie picked up the poker that was resting on the side of the furnace and began to stoke the coals just as she had done so many times before. However, this time she noticed something was very strange. Most of the coals were so soft that with a little stoking, they fell through the grate, but there was one that would not. She pushed the poker at it again and again, but it would not break up. In fact, the more she stared at it, the more she was convinced that it wasn't a piece of coal at all. It was much too big, and its surfaces were really charred and jagged.

Lizzie, carefully, positioned the poker in back of the strange object, and started to drag it toward the furnace entrance. As the object slid over the grate, it created a few sparks. As they flew up into the air, they exposed more of the strange object's shape. That's when Lizzie realized, to her horror, just what it was. It was half of a human skull.

CHAPTER THREE

A local police car sped down an unmarked gravelly driveway, and then made a sudden stop in front of Lizzie Bateman's colonial house; the front door was partially open. A shaken Lizzie stood on the porch with a furnace poker in her right hand. She was wearing only a night robe with a belt pulled tight. Her father had taught her that she should always be prepared to defend herself if anyone or anything ever threatened her. With all her years of veterinarian training and treating animals, both tame and wild, she thought she was one tough, old bird, but her hands told a different story. They twitched at different times, showing a new fear that had reached deep inside her soul.

Both of the car's doors swung open at the same time. Lizzie adjusted her glasses and took another step forward to get a better look. She could see the words "Mayfield Police" in huge letters on the side of the car as the two policemen in their neatly pressed blue uniforms approached her. She felt a sense of relief. Help had arrived.

Lizzie invited them in and slammed the front door behind them. "Can't let all the damn bugs get in, can we?"

The tallest detective began the questioning. "Ma'am, are you, Lizzie Bateman, who called us a few minutes ago? My name is Jack Hankin."

A smile grew on Lizzie's face. "Of course I am." She paused. "Why, I know you. You're Chuck Hankin's kid. Boy, you sure have grown up. You know who I am, don't you?" The detective looked rather puzzled.

"I was the one who repaired the elbow on your dog's front leg." She paused. "I think that was about ten years ago. Yes, that's right. You told me you were going into high school and wanted to play on the football team. At least, that is what you told me at the time, and I never forget a face."

Jack nodded politely. "Oh, yes, now I do remember you, Mrs. Bateman. I played left guard for two years until I ruined my knee."

"And your dog - how is she?"

"Trixie was a great dog, and I thank you for repairing her elbow, but I had to put her down last summer. She was getting too old and was not able to stand up. Her hind legs had given out."
"I'm so sorry."

The other policeman was getting a little impatient with all the chitchat, so he spoke up. "Mrs. Bateman, You called the station and said you found a human skull. Is this true?"

Jack raised his hand. He had to interject. "Excuse me, Mrs. Bateman, I am sorry. This is my partner, Hank Jackson. People often get our names mixed up. I am Jack Hankin. You can see why, can't you?"

Lizzie Bateman nodded in response and gave a small smile.

Then she faced Hank. "Detective Jackson, you can call me Lizzie. Please do. Yes, I did call you because I was shocked to find a human skull in my coal furnace this morning. How it got there I haven't a clue. I had all the doors bolted. Nobody could get in."

Hank Jackson responded with a smirk. "Don't you think the skull might have been in the coal that you shoveled in the furnace last night?"

"No, I don't. I always make sure all the coals are the same size. That way I get an even heat throughout the night."

A frown appeared on Hank's face. "Will you please show us the skull?" "Sure. Follow me." Lizzie switched the poker to her left hand, and led the detectives through the parlor and the kitchen, and down the stairs to the basement.

At once, the detectives detected a putrid smell as they followed Lizzie to the furnace.

"What's that smell?" Jack asked as he started rubbing his nose with a tissue.

"That smell is downright awful, isn't it?" Lizzie replied. "The only time I smelled anything like that was when I had to go into Dr. Sands's drug store. It was right after the firemen had found the burnt body of his dog. They wanted me to identify it as the doctor's."

"Couldn't the doctor identify it himself?" Hank asked. "The doctor was out of town at the time."

The furnace door was wide open. Lizzie rested the poker against the furnace, and pointed to the charred object that rested on the edge of the grate. "There it is, detectives, just as I found it about a half an hour ago."

Both Jack and Hank stuck their heads inside the furnace opening to get a better look.

Jack spoke first. "It does look like a charred piece of bone to me, but I am not sure what it is. What do you think, Hank?"

"I'm not sure either, but my guess would be that it is a part of the skull of some animal, maybe a medium-sized monkey."

A tired Lizzie became a little perturbed at their lack of knowledge, and shouted at both of them. "Let me tell you something, boys. I was a veterinarian for thirty-five years, and I have seen many different kinds of bones, and I know this skull is not an animal's. It is half of a human skull. I would guess she was once a young woman in her mid-twenties."

The detectives backed away and looked into Lizzie's eyes.

Hank began to speak in a monotone voice. "Young woman, you say?" Hank looked puzzled and wondered how she could possibly tell what this skull was. "When you looked at this, did you touch or move this skull at all?" Lizzie backed up a step too, even more perturbed than the moment she had been before. "I didn't touch a thing. This morning I found it resting in the center of the grate with some other coals. There was hardly any fire left, so I stoked them. All the coals fell through the grate but one, so I moved that one to the front part of the grate where I could get a better look at it. It was very hot then, but now it has cooled down. You can probably pick it up."

Jack became puzzled by Lizzie's statement. He rephrased part of the question Hank had just asked. "Did you touch the skull?"

"No, I did not. I just moved it with the poker. I *am* familiar with police procedure. I knew you would want to check it out for fingerprints, but I am quite sure you'll find it is just too burned to get any."

Jack was a little annoyed by Lizzie's flippant attitude, but he kept his cool. "Good! Our CSI team is the best in the county. Maybe, they can find some DNA?"

Hank looked at Lizzie as he tapped in the phone number on his cell phone. "We'll have our forensic investigator come here as well."

Lizzie added another clue. "Detectives, did you notice the trail of coal dust on the floor that you are stepping in right now?"

Both Jack and Hank looked down at the floor and could see their shoes had smeared some coal dust. Jack knew he had to apologize, and he also knew it would be impossible to find any shoe prints now. "Sorry, Lizzie, we'll have our team clean it up."

"Clean it up?" Lizzie looked amazed. "I never leave any coal dust on the basement floor, because I don't want anyone to track it upstairs. That concrete floor was as clean as my kitchen table. Someone was here, tell you, and made that trail of dust last night." "Our CSI team will check it out."

"Well, you'd better wipe off your shoes before you go up those steps."

Jack tried to soft-soap her a bit. "I agree with you that the shoe prints might be an important clue, but we have to proceed. I have to ask you a few more questions. I noticed that the skull looked like it had been cut in half. Do you have any axes, saws, or sharp knives?"

"Yes, I do, and you can check out all of them. They are in the shed at the end of the driveway. I haven't been in that shed for years, since my husband passed away, and, besides, I have nothing to hide."

Lizzie took a step or two backwards, and stretched her arm upward, touching the floor beam. She pulled a key out of a knothole in the wood, and handed it to Hank. "You'll need this if you want to get into the shed."

Hank nodded. "Our entire team will do a thorough search of your house and the shed as soon as they arrive." "One final question, Lizzie. You are retired, right?" Lizzie nodded. "On a cold morning like this, why didn't you sleep longer? What made you get up so early?"

"I was sound asleep when I thought I heard three gunshots somewhere between here and my neighbor's farm."

"Who is your neighbor?" Jack asked.

"That would be Judge Morris's." I woke up this morning trying to get my bearings. That's when I noticed my house was real cold. So I went down stairs to check the furnace."

"Are you sure there were three shots?" asked Hank.

"No, I am not positive. It could have been just a bad dream."

Lizzie knew she had had enough. Whether it was because of this grilling the cops were giving her or standing on her feet too long, she knew she had to sit down and relax for a while.

She walked across the basement and started up the stairs. "I am done talking for a while. I am going to my kitchen, and I am making myself a pot of tea. Do you want some?"

Both detectives declined the offer and began to follow her up the stairs. Lizzie looked back. "Shoes?"

Each cop took a handkerchief out of his back pocket and wiped the bottoms of his shoes. Jack thought Lizzie looked tired as she waddled up the final steps. They decided it was best to let her rest for a while. Lizzie went to the kitchen to fill a teapot with water as both cops started heading for the front door.

Jack stopped, and looked back while Hank opened the door. "Thanks again for your help. We should be back later today or tomorrow, depending on what the CSI team finds, with the results of any lab tests they make. We will also send a patrol unit by here every half hour."

Lizzie had calmed down. "Thanks, detectives."

Hank anxiously rushed ahead and was already opening the passenger door on the police car as Jack stepped through the doorway.

Suddenly a blur of something with gray and red streaks flashed past Jack. For a brief moment, Jack was dumbfounded.

Whatever it was, it raced into the house and leaped straight into Lizzie's arms. She dropped the teapot on the floor. Cold water spilled everywhere.

Lizzie was quick to notice, however, that it was a friendly dog; one she must have treated years ago. It was panting extra hard from a lot of running and was shaking horribly. She looked the dog over, and saw lots of bloodstains coating its hair, legs, and snout. She also found what looked like a bullet wound in its elbow area. She knew it wasn't a fatal wound, but she also knew the dog must have lost a considerable amount of blood.

As Lizzie continued to pat the dog and pull the matted fur from its face,she shrieked in horror. She realized she was holding the judge's dog, Jaspar.

CHAPTER FOUR

An unmarked van, with a red sports car tailgating it, came barreling down Lizzie's driveway and stopped abruptly behind the policemen's patrol car. A spray of dirt and gravel flew up from the sports car's front wheels as the driver jumped on the brakes and pulled hard on the steering wheel. The nose of the sports car dipped and swerved, just missing the van's rear bumper.

Three men dressed in white suits exited the side door of the van, and stared at the woman who was opening the door of the sports car. They didn't seem too happy with her driving and were about to yell something profane when they saw who she was. Standing there like a proud turkey was Joanna Selden, the police chief's daughter, who now worked for the local newspaper, the *Mayfield Times Review* .

Dan Olsen, the CSI team leader and the driver of the van, was quite angry also. He stuck his head out the door window to yell a line of profanity, but decided it was better to bite his tongue when he saw who the driver was. He did, however, decide to voice his displeasure in a calmer fashion. "That was pretty daring driving you did. You could have killed us and ruined all our hi- tech equipment. We're Mayfield's only CSI team, and I don't think your daddy would approve, do you?"

Nonchalantly, Joanna strutted past the men and offered only a comment. "He will never know, will he?"

Joanna opened Lizzie's front door and noticed the two cops, her brother, Jack, and his partner, Hank. They were studying Lizzie Bateman's every move. With skillful hands, Lizzie was very carefully treating a dog lying on the kitchen table; one end of a rubber hose was hanging out of its mouth, and the other end was attached to a metal bottle. Joanna also noticed that Lizzie's night robe was spattered with blood, as was the dog's coat.

Joanna abruptly interceded. "Well, if it isn't my brother Jack and his clone. On the job, I see." Both policemen looked back as Joanna added her next barb. "What are you doing here so early in the morning? Stopped by for a cup of tea, did you?"

Jack was usually a cool guy, but not with his sister, especially at this time of the day.

His anger erupted, and he retaliated. "Joanna, this is strictly a police matter. You lost that right to be here when you quit the force last year. Just what brought you out here to the country, anyway? Feeding the chickens?"

Joanna had to return the fire. "As a young cop who once worked for our newspaper, you still have a lot to learn. I am here because someone informed me of a 911 call that Lizzie Bateman made. No thanks to you. Lizzie is a dear old friend who has been part of our family for years. You would remember better if you attended the family holiday get together once in a while instead of chasing ghosts and pickpockets."

Hank had to move away. He was a bit annoyed but unwilling to say anything. He couldn't understand why the petty feuds existed between brother and sister. He got along just fine with his own sister.

Jack verbally attacked Joanna again. "Police work is my job now, to honor the law and put criminals in jail. I couldn't do that as a reporter. Can you do it now as a cub reporter?"

Lizzie knew that Jack and Joanna had quarreled with each other ever since childhood. She had seen both of them argue over the last cherry in a can of fruit cocktail. She also knew she was having a hard time performing the operation, so she spoke up.

"Joanna, please come over here and help me. Let the men do their job."

Joanna's arrogance started to subside a little as she rolled up her sleeves and approached Lizzie's side. "What do you want me to do?"

"Remember when you were in biology class in high school? One afternoon you came into my office and wanted to help me cauterize the menial vein in Trixie's leg? Well, this is Judge Morris's dog, Jaspar, and someone tried to shoot him. That person missed the popliteal artery but clipped a piece of the iliac vein. Jaspar has lost a lot of blood, but I think we can save its life. So I need you to hold his leg up like you did for Trixie while I clean and stitch the vein." And, please, don't let that can of ether fall off the table, or we'll all be unconscious. Besides, it's my last can."

"Sure, Lizzie, I can do that."

Jack had to get the last word. He said, in a rather poignant fashion, "Being you are an ex-cop, you know you have to make sure you do a good job on that dog. He could be our star witness in this whole affair."

Joanna didn't even bother to retaliate. She had her hands full.

Jack felt he had won this episode with Joanna, so he walked over to talk with Dan Olsen, who was carrying an electronic metering device into the kitchen.

In the meantime, Hank had moved even farther away and now stood at the front door, guiding the last of the CSI team into all areas of the house and telling them what to look for. He sent two members down the basement to inspect the skull and the area around the furnace, and the other he sent outside to police all the grounds, looking for anything out of the ordinary. To avoid the sibling rivalry if it should start again, Hank felt it was better to get even farther away.

"Jack, I am going to the shed at the end of Lizzie's driveway. I'll see if there's an axe in there as Lizzie says there is." Hank dangled Lizzie's key in plain view and opened the front door.

"Okay, but watch yourself," Jack answered.

Lizzie kept working on the dog, but she had heard Hank talking. She yelled back, saying. "You might have to jiggle the key in the lock. It sometimes sticks. I haven't used it in years. And watch out, my late husband told me he kept a revolver out there. I told him never to keep it around me. I don't like guns. They kill people."

"Thanks, Lizzie, for the advice."

The first thing that caught Hank's eye as he approached the shed was that he really didn't need a key to open the padlock. One half of the latch on the door was partly torn away with the padlock still attached to it. A crowbar lay on the ground. Hank assumed somebody must have used it to pry the latch away. He saw a blood smear near the end of the latch and thought the CSI team might be able to find a fingerprint. He pulled out a pair of gloves from his hip pocket, slid his hand into each one, and then he drew his revolver from the holster. Using his left hand, Hank slowly opened the shed door. As the door began to swing ever wider, he heard a click. Hank recognized right away, the sound of a revolver's hammer being cocked. Then, he heard the sound of someone rambling around and knocking over boxes.

"Who's in there?"

Hank heard a second click.

Bam. Phrrrrr.

A .45-caliber bullet whizzed under Hank's left earlobe and traveled all the way to the front window of Lizzie's house. In the dim light, Hank thought he saw the shadow of someone trying to climb up some stairs, maybe to a second floor. "Stop or I'll shoot!" Hank fired just once.

Either the stairs or the shadow collapsed. Hank wasn't quite sure, but the noises ceased.

"This is the police. Put your weapon down and come out with your hands up. Do it *now* ."

Jack and several others came running out of the house and down the driveway to see what was happening. Lizzie and Joanna stayed back to care for the dog.

Jack, a little out of breath, looked at Hank. "What the hell is going on here? A bullet came through the front window and almost hit one of our CSI team members."

Hank replied as he pointed to his earlobe. "Someone pried the latch away from the door with the padlock still hanging on it, and when I tried to enter the shed, I heard two clicks of a revolver's hammer. Nothing happened on the first click. Then someone fired at me, so I returned fire. I think I might have hit the person as he was climbing up the back stairs."

"Was it a man or a woman?" "I am not sure."

Hank looked again at the open door and bellowed extra loudly, saying. "Get out of the shed now or we will come in after you!" He was pissed off. The previous evening, he and his wife had celebrated their fifth wedding anniversary with a few friends. It turned out to be a late-night party. He was in bed, only an hour after the party broke up, when he received the phone call from the police station. Having gotten just a little shuteye, he knew he was tired and just plain cranky.

For a few seconds, no sounds came from the shed.

Then a whimpering voice cried out as if it were asking for mercy. "Are you the cops?"

"Yes, we are the Mayfield Police. I repeat. Come out *now* ."

"Please, please, don't shoot me. I'm coming out." There was a lot of noise, as though the person was struggling to stand up.

Jack then said. "Throw out your gun first!"

An old Colt revolver flew past the door and landed at Hank's feet. Hank and Jack could see it was in very poor shape. It looked as if the barrel was rusted and part of the handle was missing.

"Okay, raise your arms and step outside," said Jack.

"I can't raise my left arm. You wounded me there, and I am bleeding. My right arm doesn't work too well either."

"Come out as you are." Hank replied.

A young fellow, Hank figured he was probably in his early thirties, appeared at the doorway. Blood oozed out of a bullet hole in his left arm as he staggered forward and fell facedown in the dirt and gravel. Hank reached down to touch the man's neck, searching for a pulse. He was alive, but barely, and out cold.

Hank looked up and shouted. "Someone get a stretcher now!"

Seconds later, two CSI team members came running down the driveway with a stretcher. They turned the unconscious fellow over and then, carefully lifted him onto the stretcher.

Jack and Hank observed that the fellow wore dirty, ragged clothes, and smelled to high heaven. His face was lined with pockmarks, and half his hair was missing. Scratches and scars covered parts of his body. He had a tattoo on his forearm. It was a diamond with three small lines radiating out from each side. The letters "*LA*" were inside the diamond, in bold print.

One member of the CSI team told Jack and Hank that he thought the fellow was very dehydrated and malnourished and that he needed medical attention right away.

Jack nodded.

They carried the fellow to the van and placed him in it. Then they sped off to the local hospital.

Jack and Hank walked slowly back to the house, looking at the revolver Jack had picked up. "Excuse my English, but this gun is a real piece of crap. It is rusted, and look, Hank, see, the hammer guard is broken in half. It is not balanced at all. It is a wonder it didn't explode in that man's face."

"Well, it did fire once. I know. I was the target."

Jack tried to spin the cylinder, but it hardly moved. He noticed there were only three shell casings inside. "This revolver must have been lying out in the weather or in some mud hole for a long time."

"Yes. But it is still a piece of evidence for our team to investigate."

Another CSI member hurried past Jack and Hank with a small test kit, and headed for the shed. His job was to check out the door and the interior of the shed and then collect any fingerprints.

After Jack and Hank entered Lizzie's house once again, Hank slammed the front door shut. Both knew that they had a tough case on their hands, and that they needed a lot more facts if they ever hoped to solve it.

Joanna decided to hang around Lizzie's house until the police and CSI team had collected all the evidence they could find. Being she had a nose for news, she badgered Jack and Hank for information. She was the type that would not take no for an answer. She sensed there was a real scoop to be had right here: a scoop that could make her a star reporter.

Joanna looked at her Rolex and realized she would be late getting back to the newspaper office, so she decided to call her editor and explained the situation. The editor had been an aggressive, hard-nosed reporter once himself, and he appreciated Joanna's spunk and determination to get to the facts fast. He agreed to her request on one condition. She must quickly finish the research she was doing on the history of the town of Mayfield. The town would be celebrating the anniversary of its 175th year. There would be parades, and carnivals, and the newly elected mayor would give a speech to honor the occasion.

With the operation completed, Joanna helped Lizzie carry Jaspar into the living room, and laid him on a soft pillow. Both returned to the kitchen and began cleaning up the mess left on the table and floor.

Joanna began the conversation. "Lizzie, would you, please, tell me what happened this morning? I got some good information from Jack and Hank, but I would like to hear you tell your side of the story again."

Lizzie grabbed a bunch of soiled newspapers from the floor as she tried to straighten up. She wanted to cram them into a half-full wastebasket, she said. "Well, like I told the police, I heard three shots fired outside in the fields. It woke me up. I knew it wasn't deer season. I wondered what it was. That's when I realized how cold my house was. I went downstairs to check the coal furnace. I stoked the last of the burned coals and noticed one was larger and only partly burned. I pulled it toward me so I could get a better look. When I was able to see it, I was shocked. I knew it was half of a young woman's skull."

"Did you call the police right away?"

"Yes, I did, and I must admit they arrived really soon."

"Do you have any idea how the skull got into the furnace?"

"No, I do not. I keep all the doors and windows locked. No one could get in. I am sure of that."

"Okay. Did you know the man in the shed?"

"Jack described the man to me before they took him away, and, no, I didn't know him."

"The latch on the shed door was broken. Do you own a crowbar?"

"No, not that I know of."

"Does anyone have a key to your front door? Maybe a son or daughter, or a close friend."

"No, no one ever had a key except my deceased husband and my daughter, Samantha Jurvis. She moved away years ago but gave her key back to me when she returned to live in Mayfield."

A brilliant thought popped into Joanna's mind. "Do you, by chance, mean *the* Samantha Jurvis. The one who is running to be the mayor of our town?" "Yes. I am so proud of her. In the past few years she has climbed that high."

"That's wonderful. I am happy for you.""And what was the reason Samantha came home after being away for those years, may I ask?"

"She said it all happened before she got her law degree in nearby Larksburg. After graduating from Brighton Community College, she moved into an apartment in downtown Mayfield and started working in a law office. She got into a relationship with a junior lawyer, but she discovered she didn't like his manners, and decided she wanted out of the romance. She asked me if she could stay with me for a while. Of course, I said sure, she is always welcomed here. I gave her my spare house key."

"How long ago was that?"

"That was about ten years ago. She commuted to Larksburg each day, and got her law degree. She came home to Mayfield about six years ago, and bought a house on Clearwater Street, I do believe. Samantha returned to the same law office, and had that junior lawyer kicked out. Her house is a lovely rancher on the other side of Highway 11A. Now she is happily married with a wonderful husband and a cute son and daughter."

"Do you see her often?"

"She likes to bring Lindsay, her daughter, over for lunch once a month. Todd, her son, stays home with Dad."

"To summarize, you said you heard three shots, found a skull in your furnace, and saved the judge's dog's life." Joanna paused. "And the police found a derelict man in your shed. Sounds like you had a pretty exciting morning."

"Yes, I did." Lizzie was extremely tired and started to slump down on a kitchen chair. Joanna looked at the very tired woman and could see she was not up to answering any more questions. "Lizzie, I have a final question, and then I will leave you alone to rest. "What is the judge's address, and does he usually let his dog run loose at night?" "That's two questions, my dear." "I'm sorry."

"Judge Leland Morris lives a couple of miles down the road. His house has a white picket fence around it, which his wife always kept painted. There's a mailbox near the gate. You can't miss the place."

Lizzie stared toward the parlor and could see the dog sleeping on the couch. "Jaspar never leaves the judge's side. I hope nothing has happened to him."

"Thanks Lizzie, for all your help."

Lizzie leaned over with her elbows on the table and her hands holding her head. She knew she had to forget the rest of the cleanup. She arose and started to stagger back to the bedroom.

Joanna had reached the door when Lizzie made a final comment. "You sure must have taken your police training to heart."

Joanna stared back at her. "What do you mean?"

"You interviewed me better than your brother, Jack, did, but don't tell him. I wouldn't want to hurt his feelings."

Joanna turned the doorknob and opened the door. "You have my word."

CHAPTER FIVE

Joanna jumped into her sports car and sped off, heading toward the judge's farm. In exactly four minutes she applied the brakes and skidded to a full stop in front of the judge's mailbox. She couldn't help noticing Jack and Hank's police car had rammed into the judge's white picket fence. The two cops were examining the damage to the right front fender.

She flung her door open and, proudly, strutted toward them.

"Well, well, I always believed men drivers were worse than women drivers, but this one takes the cake. Two cops who were on a simple duty call and they crack up." Joanna glanced at her wristwatch, and then give a wicked smile. "It is nine twenty-one a.m. just a few hours after Lizzie's phone call. The roads are dry, and it's only a few miles away from her house." She pointed upward. "There's not a cloud in the sky, and you hit the judge's white picket fence, and mowed half of it down." She paused. "Did the sun get in your eyes, by chance?"

"Shut up, you deserter, you bitch!" Hank retorted, his eyes showing an unusual fierceness. He couldn't care if she was Jack's sister or the police chief's daughter this time. He was steaming. He had had enough of her innuendos and sarcastic remarks.

Joanna stood her ground, so Jack stepped forward to try to make amends. He took Joanna's arm and pointed it toward the judge's house. "Jo, see that smashed window over there in the judge's house? We were coming down this road when I yelled to Hank that I thought I saw someone breaking in. I pointed toward the judge's house, and Hank, who was driving, leaned over to take a look. He accidentally pulled down on the steering wheel and lost control of the car. You know how tight the steering is on cars today.

"When I looked out the car window again, the person had vanished. But don't worry about the fence. When we see the judge, we will tell him what has happened and we will gladly pay all damages out of our own pocket. Okay?"

Joanna softened a bit and offered a compromise. "Instead of having a contractor do the work, the judge should make both of you fix the fence."

"If the judge wants us to do it, we will. Okay?"

Joanna's began wondering what she could get out of this situation. "I understand, and I'll let this one pass, but only if you give me any additional information on what you know about this case that you haven't told me in the past two hours. I need to get all the news together and submit my column to the editor this morning. It has to be ready for the evening paper and TV newsroom."

Jack conceded. "We told you most everything. From our CSI team's preliminary assessments, they have determined the skull belonged to a young woman in her twenties. Lizzie Bateman was right about that. We found a pair of old boots, size twelve, in the shed with bloodstains smeared all over it, but there were no fingerprints except, possibly, those of the fellow who shot at Hank. If there was anyone else in that shed, he must have worn gloves.

"As of yet, we do not have an ID on the fellow in the shed but the CSI team did find a partial shoe print in the coal dust on the basement floor. The team reported the partial shoe print was made by a popular boot game hunters wear, probably a size twelve. They searched the house, Lizzie's car, and all the grounds around the house, and found nothing but Lizzie Bateman's fingerprints on the basement window. Is that enough for your report?"

"Yes, it is. That CSI team is sure efficient." Joanna's mind, however, wandered back to Lizzie's answers. Why hadn't she mentioned the coal dust on the basement floor? "Is the CSI team running a fingerprints search on the fellow in the shed?"

"Yes, they are doing that as we speak. We should know something by this evening."

Hank furrowed his brow. He had become quite concerned about Jack telling Joanna everything, but he also came up with an idea. "Remember, Joanna, what we tell you is our little secret. If your father ever gets wind of this, we'll probably be demoted to a desk job in the police station. Then we will never get another assignment like this one. Instead, maybe you can help us catch the person who committed such an evil murder?"

Jack picked up on Hank's idea. "So you might as well come with us and go inside the judge's house. There are no lights or disturbances coming from the house, so I would guess the burglar is long gone and, probably, ran along the Maple trees to Whiskey Creek, but maybe he left something behind that will help us find out who he is."

Hank spoke again. "Yeah, don't you think it's about time we talk to the judge and see if he is all right?"

Joanna liked their offer and followed the two cops as they stepped onto the porch. She saw that one of the small front windows was broken and noticed there were just a few pieces of glass lying on the sill. She peeked inside and saw the rest of the glass scattered on the carpet. "Jack, maybe you are wrong. The burglar could still be inside since you didn't see him run away." Jack didn't say a word as he tried the front door but found it was locked. Since the broken window was too small to climb through, all three decided to walk around the house to the back door.

They found the back door was half open and partially off its hinges. Hank slowly opened the hanging door wider and yelled to see if anybody was home. They heard nothing. Hank and Jack started to enter, with their pistols pointed straight ahead.

"Joanna, maybe you should stay outside while Hank and I do our jobs? You could get hurt."

"So could you." "What about your father? What if he finds out you were here and injured?"

"Don't worry about him. I'm a big girl now." "Are you sure you won't stay here?"

"No way, Jose. Both of you might need backup, and I still know a little karate."

"Fine, Sis, but don't say I didn't warn you."

"That burglar was one dumb ass, wasn't he?" said Joanna. "He could have come into the house the same way we did."

"Thieves are not the smartest people on the planet." Hank replied as he crept into the living room.

Jack, who had disappeared into other rooms, yelled back. "The place is empty. Nobody seems to be here. If anybody tried to squeeze through the front window, he would have had to hightail across the field to the row of maple trees that lead to Whiskey Creek."

Joanna added her thoughts. "Look at those walls. It's like this place hasn't been cleaned in ages. Look at the floor. There's dust everywhere and crap all over. The rats must have had a field day."

Jack noticed the desk drawer was partly opened. He pulled it out, and lifted something up in the air. "Is this what the judge ate for dinner? A stale sandwich? I can't even tell what kind of meat is inside." He held the sandwich closer to his nose and took a whiff.

"Ugh, its peanut butter that's hard and rancid with no grape jelly."

Joanna spied the front page of the prior day's newspaper lying crumpled up next to a sandwich wrapper. She spread it open and saw a red circle around the article she had written about possible corruption in the courts. Someone had put an *"X"* through her name. She decided to say nothing to Hank and Jack. It would be her little secret. She crumpled the paper again and stashed it in her coat pocket.

Joanna stepped over more old newspapers and walked closer to the front wall, where she stood, admiring a painting of the judge's wife. "She was a beautiful woman. I remember her from when I was a kid, and just how the townspeople loved her. She was in our Christmas parade every year." She sighed a little. "Now this is all that's left of her."

Joanna took one step back and heard glass cracking. She reached down and picked up a broken picture frame. She saw the photograph of a young woman, a woman she did not recognize. "Hey, over here, I found the photograph of a young woman. Any idea who she is?"

Jack came out of the bedroom and looked at what Joanna was holding. "I bet it is the judge's daughter, but we'll have the CSI team do some research on it. The judge sent her to a private school, so I never saw much of her after we became teenagers."

Hank shouted from another room off the main hallway. He was in the judge's solarium, and he could see all the roses showing off their beauty in the morning sunlight.

"Look at this room. It is loaded with gorgeous plants. The judge, at least, kept this area clean and beautiful."

Both Jack and Joanna were amazed and had to agree.

The trio soon walked outside and back to the front of the house and toward their parked cars. Jack took out his cell phone and called police headquarters. "Marcy, this is Jack Hankin. Would you put out an APB out on a judge Leland Morris? He is not at home, and I suspect something is wrong."

"Jack," Marcy replied. "We only put out APBs out after the person has been missing forty-eight hours."

"I know that, but there is broken glass, and there newspapers scattered on the floor that have not been read in weeks. It's a mess in here. The judge is a respected member of this town. Something is definitely wrong, and we need to find him. I'll be responsible for the APB." Marcy agreed to the request, and Jack put his cell phone back in his shirt pocket.

Joanna asked. "Wasn't the judge supposed to be at the anniversary parade next week?"

"No", "I heard he declined the opportunity to be the Grand Marshal. He told our father he had other plans."

In the meantime, Hank had walked behind the police car and popped the trunk. He removed the spare tire and grabbed the jack handle. He walked to front passenger side of the car, where he looked at the dented fender and checked the condition of the tire. The tire tread was scratched but still in good shape. He placed one end of the jack handle beneath the dented fender, and rested the center part of it on the tire. With both hands on the other end,

Hank, using the handle as a lever, gave a strong upward motion. After pulling upward a few more times, he had forced the dented fender to move a few inches away from the tire. He stood back, admiring his work, and then looked at Jack and Joanna. "See there, the fender will not rub on the tire and shred the tread off. We can get back to the station now."

"You know," Joanna said "there is something really odd about this case. I don't know what it is just yet, but the clues keep popping up, and my mind keeps trying to fit them into some sort of weird puzzle."

Jack agreed. "Yes, I am running many thoughts through my brain too, and I am finding no answers either."

Jack looked back at Joanna as he entered the police car. He said. "If you figure out the puzzle, please let us know too."

"Sure, I will," said Joanna as she raised her middle finger. "Sure, I will." Joanna walked to her sports car and watched the two lunkheads slowly disappear down the road heading back to Mayfield.

Then, as Joanna was about to open her car door, she noticed that the lid on the mailbox was not completely closed. Being the inquisitive type that she had always been, she walked around her car and noticed bloodstained lettering that was on the far side of the mailbox. Written across the judge's name was the word "*RAM*" with a big "X" struck through it.

She thought to herself, *How did the two lunkheads miss this? They need to get better training and soon. I guess I will have to solve this case myself.*

Joanna pulled down the lid and took a peek. The bright sunshine lit half of the inside of the mailbox, revealing its contents. It was another half of a woman's skull, complete with skin and hair, lying on a red-stained handkerchief. A bullet hole was visible on the forehead area. Joanna was sure it was Rachel Ann Morris's skull.

CHAPTER SIX

The Mayfield police car was slowly making its way back to the police station. The country road leading away from the judge's farm was in terrible shape. It was very serpentine and loaded with potholes, and buckled asphalt. Some local drag racers had given it the name "Washboard Lane."

Hank was steering and weaving the car from one side of the road to the other, trying his best to avoid the obstacles. He wasn't always successful, and the right front tire kept bouncing up and down and banging against the dented fender. The repetitious sounds that were made vibrated through the cabin of the car and really began to annoy Jack.

"Why did you take this road?"

"Because there is nobody on it! And I thought it would be a quicker way to the station."

"I can see why there is nobody on it. You are only going twenty-five miles per hour. Can't you try to do better avoiding all those potholes? The sound is rattling my teeth and numbing my thinking. I am in deep thought, pondering what could have happened to the other half of the skull Lizzie found."

"I am trying to avoid those potholes," said Hank, "but there are just too many of them. Even Mario Andretti couldn't avoid them. But if you think you can do better, then you take the wheel."

Hank relaxed his hands on the steering wheel. "Then I can spend *my* time thinking about the other half of the skull."

"Keep your hands on the wheel." Jack said, his voice softening a little. "Well, all I ask is that you get us back to the station before we get a flat tire. If that happens, we'll have to use the spare you filled at the gas station last night."

Hank took his eyes off the road and stared at Jack. His voice quavered as he hit another pothole." "What spare?"

Jack's voice, in turn, rose two octaves higher. "You *did* fill the spare with air, didn't you?"

"No. You said the spare was low on air. I saw you standing next to the air compressor. I figured you would fill it."

"I had a cup of coffee in my hand."

Jack, to offset his displeasure, did his comic impression of Oliver Hardy. He dangled his tie and said, "No, I did not fill it, and that's just a fine mess you got us into, Stanley."

"Knock it off. I thought I was the smart one, Ollie."

Hank rarely appreciated Jack's humor. Although some of the cops at the station said he looked like the old-time comedian Oliver Hardy, he didn't like being called Ollie, especially by his partner. Besides, he knew he wasn't nearly as fat as the real Ollie; if he were, he'd be kicked off the police force. The police commissioner disliked overweight cops.

After dodging a few more potholes, and passing an old, dilapidated barn, they approached a sharp "S" curve in the road. That small part of the road was smooth and was not difficult to travel over. Jack assumed the county work crew must have patched it the previous spring. It was just like them to miss the really bad parts.

Straight ahead they saw another police car parked behind a dirty, black pickup truck. Its sides were splattered with mud, and it was parked high up on the shoulder of the road. They could see a policeman giving the driver a breath analyzer test. The driver was a tall, well-built guy with long, scraggly hair. He was dressed in dirty blue jeans and a faded T-shirt with only the left sleeve missing. He had arms the size of Popeye's and looked downright nasty. Behind him a large brown dog sat on the driver's seat, it barked when it saw Hank and Jack's car approaching.

Hank, slowing the police car down to ten miles per hour, looked at Jack. "I think we'd better stop and see what's going on here. That cop is my neighbor, Robert Sandoz. I didn't expect he would be on duty alone. Besides, today should have been his day off. Yesterday he told me he was going fishing today."

Jack nodded. Both men knew protecting a fellow cop was always a top priority. Hank parked their police car behind the other police car. Both cops exited and walked up to Robert.

Hank spoke first. "Robert, what's going on here? Everything okay?" Robert grabbed the analyzer from the guy's hand and looked at Jack and Hank. "Yeah, everything is fine here. This guy was doing sixty miles per hour on this road. The speed limit is thirty-five. He wavered a bit when I asked him to get out of the truck, so I gave him the breath analyzer test." Robert looked at the analyzer. "He is not drunk at all."

Jack surveyed the guy who was standing next to the door of his truck. "Tell me just how you were able to travel so fast down this road? I'd bet your truck has the latest suspension, but this road is covered with all kinds of potholes."

The guy ran his fingers through his scraggly, long hair. A quirky smile appeared on the man's scarred face as he pointed to the side of the road. "See that small hill of dirt alongside of the road? That's what we call a "big berm". Off-road bikers use it all the time doing seventy miles per hour down this road. If you keep, at least, two of your wheels on it, you can go like a sonof abitch. I might add that the bikers don't get caught."

Jack could see the guy was two inches taller than he was, but still he looked the guy square in the eyes and replied. "Well, thanks for the tip, but on this road just remember the speed limit is thirty-five, just like Officer Sandoz has told you. Forget the bikers. We'll get them someday."

Jack noticed that the man's left sleeve was rolled up, while the right sleeve covered his whole arm. "Why the long sleeve?" he asked.

"My new girlfriend made me get a new tattoo. I don't care much for it, so I hide it."

Hank moved along the side of the truck as Robert spoke next.

"Hank and Jack, This is Edwin Caste."

Hank didn't look back. He was too busy looking over the truck.

Robert continued. "I have seen Edwin around town on different occasions, usually with his dog. Whenever I would ask him what he was doing, he would always say he was looking for part-time work. He says he has no particular trade other than hunting but is willing to work for food or money. He says he has a family in a trailer on the other side of Highway 11A."

Robert turned to face Edwin. "Edwin, you are free to go this time. Remember, though, next time I catch you speeding, I will have to give you a ticket."

Edwin gave them a smirk, and then, half smiling, raised his arm in the air as if to give a high five. He turned to open his truck door wider but stopped when Hank yelled. "Hold it right there, Edwin." Hank pointed toward the rear of the truck. "I see dried blood on the rear side panel. Can you tell me how it got there?"

"Yes, I can. I was out hog hunting on the land behind the judge's farm. The hog I shot was a three hundred and fifty pounder, and a tough one to bring down. It took three shots."

Jack started to ask the next question as Robert and Hank pulled back an army blanket covering the body of a huge black and gray boar with three inch tusks. Its head was matted in blood, and one eye was missing.

"Where is your rifle?" Hank asked brusquely.

Edwin opened the truck door all the way and reached under the seat. His dog stood up on its haunches and barked. "Shut up, Chopper." He pulled out a .30-6 caked with mud on the stock, and held it in front of his chest. Just as a precaution, Jack prepared himself by putting his hand on his revolver.

"Here it is." "It's my Sammy. She has never left me down."

Edwin yanked the magazine out of the rifle with is right hand, and then showed it to Jack. "You can see here. There are three missing rounds in the magazine."

"All right," "you can put the rifle back in the truck now." Robert looked at the boar again. "Edwin, that is one fine hog. The biggest I've seen in a long time. Where did you say you killed it again?"

"Down by Whiskey Creek, behind the judge's farm. It is always hog hunting season, and the judge has always allowed me to hunt on his farmland. I have my permit. Want to see it?"

"That's okay.""And you said you shot it this morning?" "Yes, sir. That I did."

"What time was that?" Hank asked.

"Oh, I get up with the chickens. I'd say it was between four and five o'clock."

Jack spoke up. "Did you see the judge recently?"

"Yes, I did, two days ago. And he told me that he was pissed off at some snot-nosed reporter digging up the history of the local court."

"Did he say what he would be doing or where he was going?"

"I think he said he was getting out of Mayfield for a few days. That's all I know."

"Thanks."

As Hank pulled the blanket further back over the hog, he noticed there was no blood on the inside of the blanket or on the truck bed. He assumed Edwin must have gutted the hog before loading.

Robert saw no need to prolong the discussion, so he proceeded to end it. He could hear someone calling on his CB and wanted to get on with his patrol. "Thanks, Edwin. You drive slower so I won't have to stop you again? Okay."

Edwin placed the rifle under the seat, pushed Chopper aside, climbed into the truck, and waved as he pulled away.

Jack and Hank walked closer to Robert. Jack agreed that Edwin seemed okay, a true outdoor hunter who liked to be on his own.

Hank, however, had a real concern for his neighbor and friend. "Robert, you know it is dangerous for one officer to be out here alone on this road. You could get seriously hurt or killed. We just found a part of a skull at Lizzie Bateman's house, and I almost got shot entering her shed."

Before Hank could continue, Robert spoke. "Thanks for your concern, guys, but my partner is in the hospital with pneumonia. My wife is pregnant, and we need the money. Besides, all I meet out here is guys like Edwin. Don't worry."

Seconds later, Robert was buckled in his car and driving away.

Jack and Hank looked at one another in disbelief, and then they climbed into their car and shut the doors. Hank started the engine and grabbed the steering wheel, ready to follow the berm and continue down the road.

From out of nowhere, a red sports car hit a pothole as it pulled up along the left side of the car. A woman with flowing hair applied the brakes, and her car pushed some of the loose road gravel against Hank's car. It was Joanna, and, as always, she seemed to be in a big hurry.

Hank lowered the power window. "What's the big rush this time? Lost? Need directions?"

"No, but maybe you do?" Joanna answered.

Jack yelled across the front seat, "Why did you say that?" "You sure know how to miss clues. The far side of the judge's mailbox held some information you should definitely have in your police files. Check it out, you ams." Joanna turned her attention to driving and sped away, and riding on the berm.

Hank, with a frown on his face, asked Jack, "What did "ams" mean?"

Jack replied, "Oh, it's really nothing. All through high school we would hassle one another. If one did something stupid, we would call that person an "ams" or lunkheads. "Ams" means "amateurs." You know what "lunkheads" means."

"Oh, I see. She said we were stupid amateurs. I'll remember that when she fouls up."

Jack felt gnawing, hunger pains. "Let's go back to the judge's place and check out the mailbox Joanna was talking about, and then, we have to grab some breakfast. My stomach is talking back to me. Afterward, I'll get a search party together and we'll scour the area behind the judge's farm, looking for any evidence."

"That's a large area, maybe a hundred acres or more."

"I know. My ass will be dragging by the time I'm finished."

Hank pressed on the gas pedal and turned the steering wheel toward the center of the road. He immediately hit a pothole. The tire tread was rammed into the dented fender, but little damage resulted. No one said anything. Hank steered the car toward the berm. Jack kept his cool and said nothing as they headed back to the judge's place.

CHAPTER SEVEN

The weather was ideal. The sky was solid blue except for a few cumulus clouds in the far west. The heat from the afternoon sun had reached its zenith. A huge assemblage of men, women, and teenagers was scouring every inch of farmland above Whiskey Creek and, especially, the judge's property. Everyone was feeling the sun's warmth, and most had their jackets unzipped. A light mist had fallen earlier, but now it was a perfect autumn day and expectations were running high they would find the judge. One man, a loner and unknown to the town folk, had his team of dogs sniffing out every possible scent.

While Hank remained at the police station, collecting all the known facts in this case and pinning them on a large bulletin board, Jack was at the forefront of the search party, making doubly sure each square inch of land was truly searched. The people were not quiet. One could hear the leaf litter crunch under each person's foot. Any animal that was in the area would have heardit and scampered to foreign ground. Together all the people sounded like a herd of hippos traveling through the underbrush.

As hours slipped by, the search party had found only a deer's antler and a hunter's old glove. The clouds were on the move when someone standing near a clump of young maple trees shouted out as loud as he could. Everyone froze.

Jack turned and rushed toward the distant person. He could see the man was dressed in a red sweater that barely covered his rotund belly and he had a corncob pipe pressed between his bulbous lips. As Jack got closer, he recognized him at once. It was Avril, who ran the feed store in town.

"You know you have a booming voice," said Jack.

Avril smiled. "I got that way from slopping the hogs on my father's farm.

Some people said I could make a great Tarzan call." "They're right. What have you found, Avril?"

Avril pointed to the disturbed pile of dry maple and oak leaves. "Look at that round hole. Someone might think that hole is a nest of some kind. Maybe a pheasant? Well, I'll tell you it isn't. See that scrapping on the dirt? That was a human hand trying to write something." Avril was known to see things nobody else saw, UFOs being one of them, but Jack knew he still had to check it out.

Jack bent down and gently pushed aside a few more leaves. He studied the dirt. With some imagination, Jack thought he could make out two letters, "AL." Jack stood up and shouted for the nearest CSI team member.

Avril took a long drag on his pipe and blew a steady stream of Prince Albert into the soft breeze. "Yes sirree bob. That's what it is."

Dan, the CSI leader, having heard Jack's shout, ran up the incline, carrying his bag of tools and a camera.

"Dan, Check out this hole while I get the man with the dogs. Maybe his dogs can pick up a scent from the leaves."

The unnamed man was standing in the crowd. He came forth, with his dogs standing off to the side. He was a complete stranger to Jack, but he reassured Jack his dogs were the best at tracking. Jack asked him for his help now that they had a possible scent.

The man agreed. He held on to the leashes but allowed the dogs to get closer to the hole.

One dog immediately yelped, and the second dog joined in.

They began pulling hard on the leashes.

"They have the scent of something, and they're eager to follow the trail."

Jack nodded, and the man released the dogs. They continually howled as they raced off past some big conifer trees. In seconds, they were out of sight. All the people headed in the same direction until Jack stopped them. He still wanted the rest of the farmland to be searched. He gave strict orders to Dan to lead them away and continue the search.

Then Jack ran to catch up to the man who had the dogs. The man couldn't run fast, and Jack quickly closed the gap. As he came up along his side, he asked the man his name.

The man replied, "Just a dog lover who was passing through town today when I heard you were getting together a search party. So I said why not. My dogs needed exercise, and so do I."

"Well, I'm glad you were in our town. We don't have a dog team like you do." "Why not?"

"Mayfield leaders say it's not needed."

"With a town the size of Mayfield and all the farmland around here, I think you should have one. Never can be too careful these days. All the crime and such."

Jack was getting a little suspicious. Who was this guy, and why was he carrying a Bowie knife on his belt?

A few minutes later, Jack and half of the search party came upon the yelping dogs.

They were jumping around a tree, acting like a gold miner who had just struck pay dirt.

The man pulled the dogs away from what looked like a tree limb, and attached their leashes.

Jack stepped closer and knelt down.

"Get a couple of CSI team members up here right now. We have a badly torn human arm, maybe a woman's." Jack could see it was in horrible shape, bearing severe gashes and deep bites. A chunk of flesh was torn away, exposing the radial bone.

Avril arrived and spoke up. "I could almost bet that a large old hog did this." In the past two years, the hog population has doubled around here. Nasty critters. I saw one as big as a pony the other day. Scared the livin' hell out of me."

Jack told the small crowd that was beginning to surround the scene to move backwards so two CSI team members could inspect the arm. After photographing the whole area, and taking critical measurements, they carefully picked up the arm and to place it in a bag. A small twig fell from between the two fingers that were still attached to the left hand.

Jack spoke. "Avril was right. Whoever this person was, that left arm has something to tell us."

Then Jack ordered a CSI member to get this evidence back to the lab at once.

Jack stood up and surveyed the people. A series of shadows started covering the sun. He looked up and saw that cumulus clouds were coming in fast. He raised his hand to get the people's attention. He knew a thunderstorm would wipe out any new evidence. "I guess we have about a half an hour before Mother Nature drowns us with her tears. Every one of you, please head back to your cars and trucks, but go a different way and keep your eyes open. We don't want to miss anything. Thanks to all of you for coming out and for your help."

Jack scanned the crowd, looking one last time for the man who offered the use of his dogs. Jack wanted to thank him for his help, but he had quietly disappeared.

Jack turned to the other CSI team member. "Go tell Dan to send the rest of the search party home. We are done here."

CHAPTER EIGHT

In the police station room, Hank was posting a photograph of a young woman on a large bulletin board when Jack moseyed in. Jack took a quick glance at the board and noticed it was filling up fast. Maybe too fast, he thought.

"Who's the woman?"

"We believe it could be the judge's daughter, Rachel. Our CSI team took preliminary measurements of the two halves of the skull, and found it matched the photograph in Rachel's old high school yearbook. The team was able to get some DNA from a piece of a tooth that was embedded in the upper jaw and also from some scalp hair. Our team found a few hairs in one of the judge's bedrooms. They are trying to match them for a positive ID. Our boss, your father, told me the CSI team has been put on high alert and is working around the clock to help us find the answers to this murder. Maybe with that new high-speed DNA processor they just installed, they can give us those results in a day or two instead of weeks."

Jack slumped down into his chair and put his feet on the desktop. He was worn out from leading the search party all day, and finding little evidence.

Hank could see the mud and wetness on Jack's shoes. "Did you find anything?" "Yes, we found a partly chewed arm. Seeing what was left of the muscle tissue and some blond hairs, Dan estimated it was from a thirty-year- old woman. When another CSI team member started to pick up the arm, a twig, possibly picked from a nearby maple tree, fell from between her fingers. We think the woman was trying to write something, judging by the scratch marks we found on the ground."

"Anything else?" You were out there most of the day."

"No, that's all we found after a long search. We covered every square inch of land except for the small stretch along Highway 11A."

"You did check the Whiskey Creek area?"

"No. That's the state's property. I called them, and they said they would conduct their own search."

"But you know how that goes with the State. They drag their feet on everything, saying they don't have the money in their budget."

"Yeah, I do know what you mean. Remember last month, when a hiker found some small body parts near Larksburg city dump, and it took the State four days before their team began to investigate the scene?"

"And Larksburg is south on Highway 11A, where the most people live in this state. You would think that town would have priority over us."

Jack reached for the can of cola that was on Hank's desk and took a long swallow. It was so cold and refreshing that it perked him up a bit.

"Hey, that's my cola. Who said you could have any?" Hank was being rather belligerent but Jack paid him no mind. He knew Hank would give him the shirt off his back, if it were necessary.

Jack looked beyond Hank's big head to survey the board once again. "You know, it's a good thing the police commissioner gave us this job. We needed some detective work. We were getting rusty, and it was getting pretty boring sitting around here lately. I was getting mighty tired of writing traffic tickets. This town has been really quiet as of late. I can feel we were stuck in the calm before a storm. Now that storm has arrived. The people around here are getting antsy about the lack of work, and hoping the upcoming election will be a blessing. The present mayor knows he has a real fight on his hands if he wants to save his job."

"Yeah, you're right. I sense the calm has passed, and now we are in a storm cloud. Did you know that this morning our outgoing mayor told the police commissioner in no uncertain terms that he expects this case to be wrapped up by the time the town celebrates the mayor's victory?"

"It will also be the town's one hundred and seventy-fifth anniversary," Jack added.

Jack looked at the calendar on the desk "That is less than a few days away. That's a lot to ask of us. Looking at that bulletin board, I'd say we have collected an awful lot of evidence in a very short amount of time, but we don't even have a real suspect, do we?" He looked up at Hank, who was holding a magic marker, and stared. "Well, do we?"

"No," said Hank, "but I think once that man who took a shot at me wakes up and can talk, we will be a lot closer to finding the judge and who the skull belongs to. I think he is the key to solving this case, not the judge's dog."

"How is Jaspar doing, anyway?"

"Dan phoned Lizzie, and she said Jaspar is going to be okay. If it becomes necessary, she would like to keep him."

"Did you get any word from the hospital on the man who tried to shoot you? What's his condition?"

"The station has had a guard posted outside his room twenty-four hours a day. That guard phoned me an hour ago, and reported that the doctors said it would be another day before the patient would be healthy enough to answer any questions. The guard also said he heard the man tossing around in his bed, whimpering, and then shouting out words, but only a few that made sense. The guard thought the words he heard sounded like "Leave my girlfriend alone." The doctors had to come into his room and put him under heavy sedation. Later the nurse told the guard she thought the man was having a strong reaction to some unknown drugs."

Hank walked over and grabbed the can of cola out of Jack's hand. "You buy your own. The vending machine is around the corner, in case you forgot." He guzzled down what was left in the can.

Jack stood up and went to the bulletin board to get a better look. He scanned every bit of evidence. "Something is strange about this case. I will say it again. We have this growing list of evidence. It's unusual to collect this much evidence in such a short amount of time. What's going on, Hank?" Hank was silent. He had no answer.

Jack rambled on. "Joanna called me while I was leading the search party, and she asked if the party had found anything. I told her about the mangled arm and possible writing in the dirt. She said she also reiterated to me she felt things were not adding up. She felt there was something strange about this case, but she couldn't quite put her finger on it either."

Both Jack and Hank had turned their attention back to the bulletin board when the police commissioner, Jack's father, strolled into their office. He was a stout ex-marine drill instructor who demanded attention. Both Jack and Joanna knew their father well. "Obey or get punished" was his motto. Even now that Jack and Joanna were grownups, he tended to run roughshod over them, but they loved him just the same.

"Did I hear you say something strange about this case?" asked the commissioner, "I hope you don't have my daughter working with you! She loves mysteries. Might I remind both of you she chose the newspaper over us? Let her sweat this case out and dig for answers on her own. Besides, I think the Mayfield Times Review is bigoted toward us. They never have anything good to say about this department. So keep your mouths shut about this case. Understand?"

Jack and Hank were aghast. "Yes, sir," they said in unison.

The commissioner was also a smart leader. He knew he must add a word of encouragement. "Keep up the good work, men."

As the police commissioner started to walk away, he turned to give a final ultimatum."I want a full report on your progress in this case on my desk by tomorrow night. The mayor wants to see it too."

As the commissioner left, Jack and Hank looked at each other. Jack scratched his head.

"I don't understand what's the rush is. Why is the mayor so anxious for us to solve this case? And why are the senior detectives in our department not helping us?"

Hank looked worried. "I wondered that myself. I think we'd better get back to work and decide what we should do next, even if it takes us all night to figure it out."

Dan Olsen strolled into the office with some papers in his hand. "I have the test results of the revolver the man shot from the barn. "The bullet we found stuck in Miss Lizzie's house was a .50 caliber. It didn't match anything we have in our database. The revolver was in very poor shape. It is a wonder it didn't explode in the man's face."

As Dan handed the papers to Jack, Hank spoke up. "Jake, do a complete background check on all the people we have listed on this board. See what you can dig up." "Our team can get on it right away."

Jake walked closer to the board and scanned the names. "You want me to check out the mayor and Lizzie Bateman too? They're good people in our community."

"Check out all of them, and do it as quickly as you can." Dan nodded and walked out of the room.

"Thanks, Dan." Hank's voice trailed off.

As both cops returned their attention to the bulletin board, Jack's cell phone rang. Joanna was calling.

"Jack, I think I'm on to something." "Joanna, what is it?"

"I can't tell you over the phone. Too many ears around here. Meet me tonight at theFlamingo Bar. Say seven o'clock. Bring Hank, my favorite lunkhead. The phone went dead.

Jack turned back to face his partner. "Hank, we have a date with a beautiful woman tonight. Put on your best duds. We're going to paint the town."

CHAPTER NINE

The day was overcast with a low ceiling of nimbostratus clouds. The temperature had dropped suddenly, and light snow showers were predicted for the entire day. The afternoon traffic on Highway 11A was moving at a snail's pace, but Alfa (Edwin Caste) could care less. He was in no hurry to get to the airport. Atlas Airlines, flight 1461 was not scheduled to land until 5:00 p.m. Alfa knew Laura Chambers was always on that flight. Alfa had nicknamed her the "Freight Freak."

Laura had grown up in Scottsville, a village about fifteen miles east of Mayfield, and her childhood desire was to become a jet pilot. In school she had read about the Greek craftsman, Daedalus, who flew with wings made of wax. From that time on Laura wished she could be soaring through the skies too. She became upset, however, when she read the sun had melted the wax off the wings Daedalus made for his son, Icarus, and she vowed she would someday fly higher and faster. Laura vowed she would never drop out of the sky like Icarus. It was not an option.

Throughout her school years, Laura had worked hard to keep her grades up while spending long nights in her bedroom flying jet planes on a video screen. In her senior year she applied for admittance to the Air Force Academy. The air force did accept her but later disqualified her for air force jet pilot training school because she did not have twenty-twenty vision. Glasses and contacts, she was told, were unacceptable at that time.

After two years of schooling, Laura dropped out of the program and decided to attend a local college. That is where she met Alfa and his friends. They would often be huddled on the steps of a frat house studying Greek literature while a wild party was raging inside. They were weirdoes, but Laura liked them. They became her friends, and she joined their secret club.

Now Laura was thirty years old and sitting in the copilot's seat of an incoming cargo plane. There were no passengers, just freight, and lots of it. Laura had worked hard to climb to her present position, but she believed the position was a dead end. She felt the company considered her only good enough only for a second-rate position, but never good enough for the pilot's seat. Years had passed with no hopes of a promotion. Carrying a grudge from her air force days, she had also come to believe only pilots with twenty- twenty eyesight were allowed to fly the prestigious passenger routes to exotic locations. But Laura never lost hope; she would persevere until someday a pilot's seat was hers. Then she could fly higher than Icarus, and be in control. As Alfa drove into the airport parking lot, he wondered why Laura had not attended their last club meeting, which was held at his house. Laura never answered her voice mail, a sure sign something was up. He felt she must have heard through the grapevine the club was disbanding, and all members were required to turn in their gold watches, inlaid with their secret names in diamonds, and their secret identification cards. What he did not know was that Laura couldn't care less. She was sorry she had ever joined such a distasteful club and just wanted out.

At 4:08 p.m. Alfa drove his black pickup truck into the airport parking lot, and stopped at the tollbooth. Inside a small fellow of Spanish descent sat on a stool.

"How much will it cost me to park here for two hours?" Alfa asked. "Mister, we charge one dollar for every half hour. Follow the signs up the ramp, but you must not park your truck in the designated areas marked with blue lines. They are for the handicapped."

Alfa became quite perturbed. "I'm no cripple, but I'll park wherever the hell I want to. You short shit Chicano."

The little man was scared but yelled back. "You do and I will call the security guard."

"This is my country, and I can do as I please. You're trespassing on America's land, wetback, and I shoot varmints like you. Now give me a ticket so I can park this piece of crap I'm driving." Alfa gunned the engine, and a big cloud of bluish smoke poured out of the tailpipe.

"Okay, here." The little man shoved the ticket into Alfa's hand and grabbed twenty dollars.

"Thanks, amigo. Here's something for your troubles." Alfa threw a black garbage bag out the side window, which landed at the little man's feet. "My wife doesn't eat anymore. She lost her appetite when she lost her soul. See ya, short shit." Alfa stepped on the gas and sped up the curved ramp that led to second-tier parking.

The little man watched the truck for a second and, then grabbed his nose and shook his head. The smell that came from the back of the truck was utterly disgusting. At first, he felt like choking, but after he pulled his shirtsleeve over his mouth, he quickly recovered. The little man bent over and opened the bag. Inside he could see, maybe, maybe thirty pounds of pork, freshly cut up. He closed the bag and called his wife to come over right away and pick up the bag.

The little man smiled and thought to himself, *"Maybe that hombre smells like mierda, but I do like pork."*

Alfa looked around the parking lot, trying to decide where to park. At the last moment he settled in a blue-lined space next to a BMW. He grabbed a brown bag off the seat and exited the truck. He looked the area over once more to see if there were any security guards around, and then he walked to the elevator. His deceased father, a felon in his own right, who had made the FBI's most wanted list twice, had taught Alfa that anyone in a uniform was fair game. To Alfa that meant the hunting season was year-round with no bag limits.

Alfa hurried across the parking lot to an elevator. He could see an elderly couple was trying to through the closing elevator door. He pushed them aside and squeezed inside the car. He pressed the button for the third level. The elderly couple's son, who stood in back of the car, stared at the crude and unkempt man but dared not say anything. He could sense Alfa was no man to deal with.

The elevator door opened, and Alfa headed straight to a steel door marked "Personnel Only." Alfa rapped on the door, and it opened. A security guard appeared. Alfa presented his fake security badge. The guard scanned the card, and said he would allow Alfa to enter if he told him what was in the brown bag. A cheerful Alfa opened the bag, and stated it was a gift for a celebration with a dear old friend he hadn't seen in months. He added that they had gone to the same college, and shared a love of flying.

The guard stepped aside and allowed Alfa to enter.

He hurried down a long hallway to the lounge room, hoping no one would be there. When he opened the door, Alfa could see the place was empty except for two pilots standing by a table, discussing a flight plan. They seemed about ready to leave, so Alfa opened a cabinet door above a sink and found two plastic glasses. He sat down and waited. Alfa had met Laura once before in this lounge room, and knew Laura always came in after her flight. He looked at his watch. It was 5:15 p.m. He knew there were some things he was willing to wait for.

Laura walked into the lounge room pulling a wheeled cart containing her luggage. She seemed surprised to see Alfa sitting alone. She walked over, placed her cart beside a chair, and sat down.

Alfa appeared to be in a very friendly mood. "Hi, old friend. Care for a drink?" Laura asked. "What are you doing here? It isn't often you come to the airport. Is something wrong?"

Alfa poured an expensive scotch into each glass. Then he dropped two ice cubes in each glass. "Here's a stirrer. I know you like yours stirred."

"Thanks for the drink. What's the occasion? Is Libby pregnant again?" Laura stirred her drink, took a sip, and waited for an answer.

"No, nothing like that. She's on a long vacation. I am here because I thought we would celebrate an anniversary."

Laura took another sip and placed her half-empty glass on the table. Alfa promptly refilled it. "What anniversary are you talking about?"

Alfa tried to evade the question, at least, for a little while to give the poison time to set in. "You know, this is the most expensive bottle of scotch I could find. It cost me two hundred bucks. I could have bought a new rifle or an old whore for that. But you are special. You were always friendly, from the time I first met you in our secret college club. You helped me get on my feet, and I will always be grateful. You know as well as I do that I am a real son-of-a- bitch who does a lot of bad things and will continue to do them. I'm a bad ass. I think it's an addiction, like taking drugs. But I wanted you to know I consider you my friend. Enough said."

Laura repeated her question. "What are you talking about? Anniversary? Where are you going with this?"

"Laura, the anniversary we are celebrating is the seventh year of Leonard and Rachel's life in the concrete cave."

"Leonard and Rachel? I thought you would have let them go by now. They must be like caged animals. Hasn't it been long enough?"

"They are not going anywhere. Both of them are dead."

Laura was stunned. "What happened? Did you kill them like you did that poor, innocent security guard? A crime all of us in the club witnessed?"

"Yes, Laura. You are right. I am the cleanup crew, all in one. I have been assigned to dispose of all evidence, including you."

"Uh...." Laura felt a tightening in her throat.

"Don't try to say another word. The poison I put on your stirrer reacts quickly. You are being paralyzed, starting with your vocal organs. Don't move, and you will live a little longer? Maybe five minutes. I'll be here to assist you."

Laura stared at Alfa in disbelief. She could feel her life slipping away, and she could do nothing about it. Now she wished she had told the police the truth. She could see the madman sitting across the table, patiently waiting and watching. A broad smile was plastered on his face.

Alfa took a long sip of his scotch and pulled out a big Cuban cigar. "See this, Laura? This is my reward for a job well done. Omega and I are a couple. We are going to be the last members of the club. Tonight we are going to celebrate the deaths of Leonard, Laura, and, of course, that pretty little thing, Rachel. Tomorrow Johnny will meet his end too. Again, thanks for all your help. "Omega and I are free from worry about those shitheads we had to keep in the hole in the ground, and now we can live our lives in comfort and freedom. So long, good friend."

As Alfa got up to leave, Laura, having lost all feeling in her arms and torso, turned her head, and winkled her eyebrows in a sneering way. She was trying the best way she knew how to say to Alfa, "Screw you!"

CHAPTER TEN

Mother Nature was touching Jack and Hank with an early dusting of snow as they entered The Flamingo Bar. A rowdy group of lumberjacks sat at the bar, reveling about how many trees they had cut down that day. The bartender, however, seemed quite indifferent to their fun. He kept wiping the countertop in a deliberate fashion, waiting for someone to order the next beer. Nearby a couple of young cowgirls dressed in halter-tops, shorts, and high heels were romancing a young man who was trying to shoot a game of eight ball. Off to the right side was the dining area, where a loving couple was toasting one another with glasses of wine.

Because the ceiling lights grew dimmer toward the back of the room, Hank and Jack could barely make out who was sitting at a small table not far from the rear door. As they approached the table, they could see Joanna was holding up a half-empty glass. It was probably her favorite, an apple vodka martini.

Joanna glanced around the room, checking out her surroundings, and then focused on the two policemen sitting down at her table. "I see you didn't wear your uniforms tonight, probably because you didn't want them to get wet from the snowflakes you are covered in. This is a small town. Everybody around here knows who you are, with or without your uniforms."

Jack brushed a few snowflakes off his jacket as he faced his nemesis. "Very funny. Now can you tell us what was so important you couldn't tell us on the phone? What could possibly be the reason you asked us to meet you here?"

Hank piped up. "You'd better have something good for us. My wife is waiting for me at home with a candlelight dinner."

"Hold on to your britches." She paused.

A cocktail waitress strolled up to the table. She had a white ten- gallon hat and a pair of fake revolvers on her sides; her breasts were pushed up in her haltertop to exaggerate their fullness. She offered an alluring smile and asked if anyone wanted a drink. Hank ordered a light draft beer, and Jack said he would have bourbon and water, not stirred.

With a tip of her hat and a wiggle of her ass, she sauntered off.

Joanna shook her head. "Doesn't she know not to make a play for two cops?"

Hank was anxious, as always, to know the news. "Tell us what you have."

Joanna was just as anxious to tell what she had found. "This is what I have for you." You know I have to do an article on this town's history for the one hundred and seventy-fifth year celebration."

"Yes, we are well aware of that." Hank leaned forward, looking dead serious. "Keep going."

"This afternoon I was in the *Times Review* basement, digging through some old history files. I found a lot of them were water ruined. I hope someday when the newspaper gets extra money in the budget they will computerize what is left of all those files. But for now they're in a dead space, faded and dusty. I asked around the office, and nobody seemed to care about them or even knew they existed. I have begun to search through every box of papers. It's a massive job, but I have found some interesting things so far."

"Okay, so what did you find that can help us crack this case?" asked Jack. "In one of the boxes I found an odd folder about a court case that happened seven years ago. The folder was worn like someone had read it many times, and was trying to hide it. In that folder I found the transcript that a typist must have taken regarding a very serious felony case. And guess who the judge was presiding over the trial?"

"Who?" Hank leaned closer to the table as two snowflakes fell from the tips of his eyelashes.

"Not Judge Lillian Baxter, who was scheduled to handle the case, but the Honorable Judge Leland Morris, that's who! He specifically asked for that case. And that's not all. It was a cold-blooded murder case, and a man named Leonard Anders was on trial for his life. The judge went against court policy. He set the bail money at fifty thousand dollars. The prosecutor was greatly annoyed, and Judge Morris almost held him in contempt. The prosecutor had requested five hundred thousand dollars because he believed the man who was being charged was a definite flight risk. Ten years ago he was arrested for grand theft auto, and tried to skip town. The miffed judge would hear none of it and replied with a loud no to the district attorney's request."

The waitress returned with their drinks, but when she saw she was being ignored, she placed the check on the table and hurried off.

Joanna was just getting warmed up. "So I started digging deeper and found a tiny article in the gossip page of an old newspaper dated the same day. The rumor mill had it that the judge's daughter, Rachel, was secretly in love with Leonard Anders, the man on trial."

"Just out of curiosity, I went to my personal computer and checked out the judge's bank accounts during that time period. He did withdraw fifty thousand dollars from his savings account, and from all indications he didn't spend one penny on any large commodity. He drove an old rusty Chevy sedan for years when he could have bought a new one. In all my digging, there is simply no record or receipt showing he bought a big-ticket item. None."

Jack was taken back. "Wait a minute! Are you telling me you hacked into the judge's banking accounts? Are you insane? You know that is a serious criminal offense, don't you?"

"Arrest me, bro. You want to solve this case, don't you?""My gut feeling is that the judge found out about his daughter's romance and tried to stop it, but she must have used her charm to sway him. Remember, she was his only child. From the celebrity pages, I could see she must have been a daddy's girl who could do no wrong. Rachel must have made him take fifty thousand dollars from his savings account so she could use it for Leonard's bail money."

Hank spoke next. "Did you find any evidence to support this idea of yours?"

"No, I did not. However, this is strange. After the man was released on bail, he disappeared, and Rachel disappeared as well. A search party combed the entire county for days, and an APB was issued, but to no avail. They simply disappeared off the face of the earth. And get this. The judge never offered a reward for any evidence leading to the capture of the man and his daughter. Within a few weeks the whole thing seemed to vanish from the news media. I think the judge was pissed off at his daughter for getting him involved."

"How long ago did all this happen?" Hank asked. "I repeat, seven years ago."

Jack interrupted. "So you think, maybe, the judge knew something and went after them now, seven years later."

Joanna lifted her full glass of vodka. "Sounds like a winner to me."

Both Jack and Hank's phones rang at the same time. Joanna saw an opportunity. She got up quickly and excused herself. As she headed for the ladies' room, she noticed that the two cowgirls had given up on the young man at the pool table. The young man, in turn, spied Joanna, and tried to make a play for her. Joanna imitated a pissing sound as she, nonchalantly, walked past him and planted her middle finger in his face. "No dice, junior."

Hank listened to the message he was receiving from the CSI lab while Jack listened to a police message. Both hung up about the same time and looked at each other. A smile crossed their faces. They took long swigs of their drinks as Joanna returned to her seat.

Jack spoke with a dash of sarcasm. "That was quick. Did you forget to wash your hands again?"

"Very funny, Mr. Clean."

Hank tried to stop the insults. "Joanna, can you tell me again the name of the man who jumped bail? What did he look like?"

"According to the newspaper article, Leonard Anders was about five feet ten inches tall, slender build, and had a chin goatee. He also had a tattoo on his right forearm."

"His name again, please."

"His name was Leonard J. Anders."

"Leonard J. Anders?" Hank almost dropped his cell phone. "Our CSI lab just informed me they ran the fingerprints of the man I shot in the shed and got a hit on the FBI fingerprint database. Dan said his name is Leonard J. Anders." Hank sat back in his chair. He smiled, and took another large swig of his drink.

He believed they had the bastard who had tried to shoot him at Lizzie's shed, and the one who must have killed Rachel Morris.

Before Joanna could speak, Jack said, "Great, Hank, you have one more piece of the puzzle. I just found out the police department received a phone call from an Oscar Coyne, the pawnbroker on Third Street. He said a man walked into his pawnshop with a .357 Magnum revolver that he wanted to sell. Oscar said the man would not give his name but he could hear his dogs barking outside. The man said he was passing through town and needed some extra money. He seemed to be in a big hurry so Oscar bought the revolver. Oscar thinks it might be stolen. He wants us to come over now. He says he will stay open another hour."

Smiles crossed the lips of all three people.

"Well, boys, you'd better be going." Joanna said. "And Hank, you don't want your dinner to get cold. I understand you don't like cold food or leftovers."

"Who told you that?" He glanced at Jack. "I love cold beer, and macaroni and cheese that's been reheated."

"Sure you do. Say hello to the missus for me." "You want to come along?" Jack asked nicely.

"No, Thanks for the offer, but I need to get back to my office. I have a lot of typing to do and a ton of boxes still to go through."

CHAPTER ELEVEN

Johnny Desario was a man of short stature, but he was a gifted entertainer with a suave appearance. He had sleek, dark hair styled like the men in the fashion that was popular among men during the Roaring Twenties, a tailored black tuxedo, and black shoes with white spats. He was a generous person who enjoyed his profession and was willing to help any soul trying to make it to the top.

Johnny did look a little nervous as he appeared on the left side of the stage. Earlier in the day he had a premonition, a feeling, he would call it, that something was about to happen in his life, something not good. He wanted to call in sick, but he knew better. The show must go on.

He swallowed hard as he walked to the center of the stage and faced an unruly audience. He looked out toward the rear seats to see if the place was full, and if one tough Irishman, the owner of the club, was watching. He could, definitely, see there was standing room only, and yes, there he was. That tough Irishman was standing behind the last row of seats, puffing on a fat cigar. The man's dark receding hairline and chubby face, had always caused Johnny to think he could have been Al Capone's double.

Then Johnny looked down at men in the front row, who were acting like wild zombies. He shook his head. He offered them a half smile, but his experiences told him this crowd was going to be very hard to handle, and he was well aware there was not much he could do about it. Johnny knew the Irishman would always insist on him doing the show. He also knew this job was his main livelihood. No show, no paycheck, no condominium. It was as simple as that.

Johnny swallowed hard a second time, and then lifted his right arm, hoping for a little silence. He raised the volume of his voice also. "Gentlemen, and any ladies that might be present." A small snicker arose from the crowd. "Tonight, right here in Larksburg, the "Down and Under Club" is proud to present that international star of exotic dancing and acrobatics, the only performer alive, who uses two poles in her act because she says one just won't do. The one who has won many awards and was recently presented a Humanitarian medal for promoting Pilate's and other indoor exercises to the poor in African countries." He paused. "I wish I was poor."

"Cut the crap," One of the zombies in the front row yelled.

A bald-headed chap with frog-like eyes and large lips chimed in. "We want to see April and touch her big boobs."

Johnny took a deep breath. He thought he was used to hecklers, but their insults still made him feel uncomfortable. "Yes, and now, without further ado, here she is, straight from her grand African tour. The one and the only, Miss April Daze."

A roar came from the crowd that was so loud it could have broken a sound meter, if there had been one present. It looked as though pandemonium was about to erupt. The men of all ages had been primed and ready for the show. Hired attendants could see the potential problems and rushed forward to guard the stage.

Johnny Desario, raised both arms and clapped his hands as the curtains opened. He turned and quickly walked off the stage. The riotous crowd of half-drunken men joined in, clapping so hard, that no one could hear the music. April's small band sitting to the right of the stage was playing her theme song, "You Light up my Life," but no one seemed to be listening or caring. The first two rows of zombies were so anxious to see April and her entourage of half-naked ladies strut to the front of the stage, that their excitement had caused bulges to grow in the zipper areas of their pants.

April, a tall redhead with devilish eyes darkened in black eye shadow, and a suggestive smile, knew she could tease and entice any male, and she made no bones about it. Using her sensual body with its perfect curves, and real (not silicone) breasts topped with pink nipples, she could gyrate and slither up and down both poles in unbelievable ways. She could send men into a state of sheer ecstasy.

Some of the audience members yelled their pleasure, while others kept trying to leap onto the stage. Two older gray-haired businessmen pointed their middle fingers at April in hopes she would see them. Five attendants sporting huge biceps and small waistlines were constantly acting as a buffer. Their orders were to allow no one to climb onto the stage unless April offered that person an invitation. Two of the attendants walked over to the two gray- haired gentlemen, grabbed them by their collars, and pushed them back in their seats. With the crowd being ever so raucous, it might have looked like a losing battle for the Down and Under Club, but the attendants were doing their job quite well.

The Down and Under Club was jumping with so much excitement and noise that no one paid any attention to Johnny. In an instant he had become the forgotten celebrity, and he knew it. Before the show the Irish boss had told him he was not allowed to sing, but rather just to be the master of ceremonies. It was April's show. Johnny was depressed. Being oversensitive, he felt no one cared. Even the friendly night guard paid no mind to him. For the next forty-five minutes, Johnny would have to listen to that cacophony of sounds: whistles, shouts, and outright debauchery. He wanted to hide, and pretend he was on a desert isle, alone with nature. He moved farther away from the stage, crunched himself up into a ball in a dark corner, and covered his ears with his hands. Every time this show went on, Johnny would remember the past. He would imagine being in college, and hearing the security guard's voice. He could see the security guard lying on the ground with two bullet holes in him, pleading over and over for mercy. Then those awful sounds of three more shots being fired into his heart. Johnny Desario could not forget that terrible scene he had witnessed seven years ago, and now it was constantly torturing his soul. He prayed each day for some kind of relief, but none was forthcoming. Drugs helped only a little.

April Daze had been Johnny's live-in years ago, before she hit the big time. Then, one day, she left him high and dry without so much as a word or a thank-you. She had used him to advance her career, and he knew it. When many of the theater scouts and bigwigs came into the club, Johnny would introduce them to her. They, in turn, liked her act so much that they promoted her career with large sums of money. Soon April Daze's photos were appearing on the covers of various magazines and she was being offered videos to do, and screen tests for Hollywood movies. She even had a tryout for a Broadway show.

Johnny, on the other hand, never seemed to get that one big break he so desperately wanted in the entertainment industry. Now in his early thirties, he emceed and sang at local bars and weddings. Nothing big. Therefore, he had grown quite jealous of April's success and thought he might want to get revenge. He was willing to try anything to undermine her fame and career. Maybe, he hoped, she would see the light, and come back into his arms for good. Being a college dropout who had studied Greek philosophy, he realized his ardent love for April was starting to foster an obsession, a bad obsession. He was frightened because this was one obsession that a college course didn't teach, and he did not know how to control it. What Johnny didn't know was that his obsession would be corrected quite soon. He would never have to fret over April Daze again.

The lustful eyes of the audience focused on April's anatomy as two of her naked stage dancers began to strip her bare to the timing of the music. As every dainty piece of apparel was removed, the crowd gasped. April heard this and always knew what to do next.

She kissed the two dancers, grabbed both poles, and did a backward split, showing the symmetry of her buttocks. She turned her face toward the audience, sucked on her forefinger very slowly, and then gave the crowd her patented sly smile.

The crowd, like a bunch of cheerleaders at a high school football game, yelled with delight and asked for more. April obliged. She climbed both poles again, and slithered around each one before touching the stage. She had remarkable strength in her arms, legs, and torso and could do impossible feats. With one hand she pulled herself up one pole and wrapped her legs around the other. Then she relaxed her hands and hung by her feet. She was a bodybuilder, a gymnast, and a stripper all in one. She waved to the crowd, and they approved heartily.

The show was nearing its completion when the night guard tapped Johnny on the shoulder. The guard told him a friend was waiting outside the back door. He said the friend wanted to see Johnny right away. It would only take a minute, he said, but it was important.

Johnny Desario stood up and wiped his eyes with his hands. "Do you know who it is?"

"No, but he said he went to college with you."

Johnny knew he should go to the dressing room to check on his appearance before going back on stage. But first, being curious, he wanted to know who was waiting for him. He hurried down the short flight of steps to the back door.

He pressed on the locking bar and opened the door. No one was there, so he decided to step outside. Wearing just his light tuxedo, Johnny started shivering in the chilly nighttime air. He could see the alley was empty except for a black pickup truck that was parked a half a block away next to a small snow bank. He decided to take a couple of steps and get a closer look at the truck. He could see there was someone sitting inside the cab?

"Come on over, Phi."

Johnny was not sure he recognized the voice, so he again started cautiously walking toward the pickup truck. As he went closer, he could see a man with long hair, lowering the window. A streetlight revealed traces of his face. That's when Johnny knew who it was. It was Edwin Caste, or Alfa, leader of the club.

Johnny was surprised. "Well, hello adelphos. What brings you out here? Couldn't sleep? The second show will start in ten minutes. Did you want to see April do her thing? Is that why you are here?" Johnny waved in the direction of the back door. "It's damn cold out here. Come on in. I'll get you in for free."

Alfa didn't budge. He wanted to talk. "It's real good seeing you, Johnny. It's been quite a while, hasn't it?"

Johnny was shivering, but he said, "Yes, it really has. How have you been these days?"

"Sorta kicked my old woman and her kid out of my trailer last month. Couldn't stand her yappin' about every little thing I do or don't do. Wanted to shoot her but thought better of it, at least for a short while. Been hunting lately and killed a couple of boars behind the judge's farm near Whiskey Creek." Alfa tilted his head toward Johnny. "What have you been doing? And why haven't you been attending our club meetings?"

"I have a lot of things on my mind." "I have had some losses in my life. Some ups and downs. But I can't complain."

"You mean April, don't you? That bitch. She would screw anybody who had money."

"Please don't say that. I still love her."

Johnny could sense something was brewing in Alfa's mind, and he was getting really nervous just thinking about it. He also knew it was about time for him to go back on stage.

Alfa posed a question. "Ever think about that night we zapped that security guard?"

"We? It was you who pulled the damn trigger. And, yes, it's been on my mind quite a lot, especially since I read Judge Morris is missing. How could anybody forget it?"

"Well, I am sorry to hear about that. I was hopin' you would have forgotten about it by now. It's been seven long years, and it still bothers me. Leonard was a good friend."

"Bothers me too. I should have put two more bullets in that security guard's brain, if I'd had them."

"That damn female reporter who just started for the Mayfield newspaper is digging up old news' and she is going to find all of us guilty too. Do you want that?"

Alfa snickered. "I might have to plug her too."

Johnny took a step back. He was getting really squeamish, and Alfa could see it.

"Are you coming to our next meeting?" Alfa asked.

"No, I won't be able to make it. I have a gig that day at the Flamingo Bar in Mayfield. By the way, how are Leonard and his girlfriend doing? Do you still have them imprisoned in that concrete cave of yours?"

"They're not imprisoned; they are…"

The night guard opened the back door and yelled, "Johnny, better get in here. April is doing the last part of her act."

Johnny looked at Alfa and tried to make a graceful exit. He looked back as he started walking away. "Gotta go. It's damn cold out here, and the show must go on. If you decide you want tickets, give me a call."

"Right on, Johnny, I'll do that."

Alfa lifted the .44 Magnum with a silencer off the seat, and pointed it at Johnny's back. Johnny never knew what hit him.

"See you, in the next life, adelphos, if there is one. Your membership in our club has just expired."

Alfa blew at the tiny puff of smoke trailing out of the barrel of his weapon. He climbed out of his truck, flexed his big biceps, and lifted Johnny's body with greatest of ease, and heaved it into the bed of his truck. Seconds later, he pressed the gas pedal to the floor, and sped away. Alfa had done his job, just as ordered.

CHAPTER TWELVE

Twenty-four hours went by with no new evidence. Jack and Hank thought they might be able to take a breather. The weather was becoming colder and gloomier. An early winter was coming on fast, and the people of Mayfield were wearing their heavy attire. Hank, once again, was facing the front of the bulletin board, reiterating aloud the statements the pawnbroker had given them when Jack's desk phone rang. It was Geri, the head nurse, calling from the hospital. A little smile sneaked crossed Jack's face. He tried to hide that he liked her a lot. He reveled in the soft and gentle quality of Geri's voice; she never seemed to have a harsh word for anybody. What a difference from the people in the house he had grown up in. She kindly informed him that the wounded man in room 312A was conscious and alert and was willing to talk, and that he would try to answer any questions the police might have.

Jack replied with a polite thank you and hung up the phone. He sat still while Hank continued to outline what he thought should be their next course of action. Jack knew, that sitting in silence, and feigning an air of indifference, as though he were daydreaming, would annoy Hank to no end. He knew that Hank, ever the eager beaver, worked fast trying to understand clues and solving cases. Sometimes his speed would make him jump to wrongful conclusions, Jack had had to bail him out more than once, he liked to tease Hank about this.

Finally, Hank could stand it no longer. He had had enough. He turned to face Jack and said, "Who just called?"

"Oh, it was nothing much." Jack said, trying not to break into a smile. "The hospital just called to say that the man who took a shot at you is now strong enough to answer our questions."

Hank's face reddened, showing his annoyance. "Were you ever going to tell me? "Here I am babbling about what our next course of action should be when you already knew what it is."

"Oh, Ollie, I like to see that little wrinkle form on your forehead." Jack rose from his seat and started for the door.

"Wait a minute, pal. At least let me finish my thoughts on the revolver Oscar the pawnbroker gave us a couple of nights ago. And for your information, my wife was pissed off at me because I keep coming home so late. She almost threw the pot of spaghetti sauce in my face. If that matters at all to you, *Stan!*"

Jack reached for his jacket, which was hanging on the coat rack. "Go ahead. Don't let me interrupt you. Let's hear your spiel. I'm all ears."

"So was Dumbo, the elephant."

"I have in my hand a report from our crime lab team that I would like to tell you about. They have managed to read the serial numbers that were partially filed off the revolver Leonard had in Lizzie's shed. The lab said it belonged to a day laborer named Tito

Mangano. He lives in Mexico, and has not been in the USA for the past four years. Our crime lab said the revolver had been fired only once."

"Fine. What does the crime lab say about the revolver that the pawnbroker had?"

"Oscar told me, if you remember, that he didn't know the man who sold the revolver to him, but that he had seen him carrying a heavy backpack, and walking around the town with his dogs."

Jack became excited. "Dogs, you say? What kind of dogs?"

"Why are you not concerned with the heavy backpack?" Hank asked. "Forget the backpack. It means nothing. It's the dogs I am interested in." "Oscar said he thought they were bloodhounds because they always had their noses to the sidewalk, sniffing at everything."

Hank stared at Jack. "And when did you ever become so interested in dogs? You told me you wouldn't want any animals in your condo because they leave hair all over the place and shit in the corners."

Jack lowered his right hand in a slow motion. "Calm down, Hank." A man with a pair of dogs helped us in our search on the judge's farm. He said he was just passing through our town when he saw the search party forming and decided to help us, which he did."

"Don't you think we should question that man?" "That would be a good idea."

"Well, Jack, it's already been done. A state trooper, while on patrol along Highway 11A, stopped our suspect. The reason for stopping him was a burned-out taillight. He thought the driver of the old pickup was nervous, so he started doing a search while asking the driver a few questions. The driver was frightened. He grabbed a piece of paper out of the glove compartment and handed it to the officer. It was a bill of sale. When questioned, he said his dogs found the revolver on the far bank of Whiskey Creek. The officer returned to his patrol car and did a check on the license plate. Everything was in order. Since the man had no prior record, the state trooper agreed to let him go as long as he replaced the taillight."

Then Jack zipped up his jacket in haste. "That's just great. First, we believe we have the murder weapon, then we don't. Now we think we might have the murder weapon, but still no bodies. We have lots of circumstantial evidence to a crime, but no suspects. We are still batting a big zero in my book. Did the crime lab test the revolver for fingerprints and bloodstains?"

"Yes, they did, and there were no bloodstains, but there was a smudged fingerprint."

"Did the policeman get the man's driver's license?"

"No, he did not."

"That's just great." Jack pulled up the collar of his coat. He dropped his shoulders. "Ah shit, let's go to the hospital, and see if our wounded man can enlighten us." Jack punched the CSI numbers into his cell phone.

"Hello, Jack, what can I do for you?" asked Dan.

"Dan, remember the man with the dogs when we did a search for Judge Leland?"

"Yes."

"I didn't get his name. See if you can find out where he is staying today, and question him about the revolver he gave to the officer."

"I'll get right on it."

"Oh, Jack, I think you and Hank will be interested in this report I just received from Larksburg. The coroner's office in Larksburg is investigating the remains of, at least, three bodies found by a worker in the local dump. There hasn't been a murder in Larksburg in three years, so they wanted to know if anybody had been reported missing in the Mayfield County area."

"Thanks, Dan. Call them back, and tell them we will be at the dump tomorrow morning." Jack closed his cell phone, ready to inform Hank as to what Dan had said.

Hank forced a smile. His mind was elsewhere. "And I bet you can't wait to see that nurse you have been wishing to date for the past six months. Ah, what's her name?" Hank scratched his head. "Oh, yes, it's Geraldine, but she likes to be called Geri."

"Shut up, Ollie, and get your coat on. I am driving, remember, and I don't like backseat drivers even if they are sitting up front. If you are good, I'll tell you what Dan just told me."

"What?"

The snow was falling like one big white sheet. It was heavy and wet, which was great for making snowballs and building snowmen, but it made driving extremely hazardous. Fortunately, the long entrance to the hospital was being constantly cleaned by a giant snow blower, which the hospital had bought that year for such an occasion. A sturdy middle-aged man dressed in a red parka sat at the controls and seemed to enjoy the large amounts of snow that kept collecting on his head and shoulders.

Hank pulled the police car up to the front entrance right behind a silver luxury car. The pavement was dry thanks to the large roof that cantilevered off the front end of the hospital. A young nurse was helping an elderly woman get out of a wheelchair and into the front seat of her new Cadillac. She looked up as Hank and Jack passed by and watched them head toward the lobby doors.

She looked up at the nurse. "The tall one is cute. Nice ass, don't you think?"

The nurse smiled. "Missus Grady. They are too young for you." "I can still look, can't I?"

Once inside, Hank and Jack took the elevator to the third floor. A smiling Geri was there to greet them. She led them down a hallway to room 312A. The police guard rose from his chair, acknowledged them, and then sat down. All three entered the doorway and stood before a curtain.

Geri advised Hank and Jack in a strict but soft voice. "The man seems to be regaining his health, but he does have sudden outbursts of anger. Something is troubling him, and I think it is deep inside his subconscious. But he says he wants to talk to you, so be careful. I will be right outside the room with the guard. I will have a needle loaded with a new powerful sedative, Dyneparide, if it is needed."

Jack nodded as Hank pulled the curtain aside.

The man in the bed looked a lot better than he had when they saw him fall out of Lizzie's shed. He had lots of bruises on his chest, but good skin color in his face and neck. His eyes looked alert. Both arms were in casts, which puzzled the detectives. They knew Hank had shot him in only one arm.

Jack spoke first. "Mr. Anders, I presume. We are with the Mayfield County Police. My name is Jack Hankin, and this is my partner, Hank Jackson. We are here to see how you are doing."

Leonard Anders nodded in approval. "I am doing a lot better."

An eager Hank jumped into the conversation and started his questioning. "Do you feel up to talking to us and answering some questions?"

The man's voice rose in volume and sincerity. "Yes, yes, I do. The past seven years have been hell, one terrible ordeal. They were very painful to Rachel, my love, and I want to come clean. I will tell you everything."

Jack wondered what the seven years was all about but decided to start with the easy stuff first. "Are you Leonard J. Anders?"

"Yes, I am."

"Do you remember being in a shed and taking a shot at my partner, Hank?" "Yes, I do, and I am sorry. Please forgive me. I was out of my mind. I was battling severe headaches. I thought Alfa was coming back to kill me just like he said he would do to all the others."

"What do you mean by "all the others"? And who is Alfa?" Jack was concerned. Could this case be the work of a serial killer?

Leonard raised his hand.

"Please listen to me closely because sometimes I know I go off my rocker.

I think it was the damn drugs Alfa was feeding me each day."

"Who is this Alpha anyway?" Hank asked.

"Wait a minute. Let me catch my breath, and I will tell you the whole story." Leonard took a deep breath and tried to control his nerves and mental state, but he could feel a bout of hysteria coming on. "Alfa is Edwin… somebody. I can't remember his last name. Seven years ago I was about to be tried for murder. Alfa fatally shot a security guard on the college campus. I was framed. I admit I was involved. I didn't kill him, but I saw who did. It's just that, at the time, nobody wanted to believe me. I had a record for DUI, and grand theft auto. I admit I was young and foolish. When I checked the dying man's pulse, my fingers were covered in blood."

"Rachel Morris, Judge Morris's daughter, who I loved with all my heart, believed in me. She convinced her father to reduce my bail to fifty thousand dollars, which he did. Rachel also convinced her father that I was innocent and she loved me. She begged her father to take fifty thousand dollars out of his savings so she could bail me out. She believed she could find a good lawyer who would get the jury to find me not guilty. But more evidence kept piling up against me every day. My so-called friends at college, and neighbors at home gave the police a bad report on me."

"Why is that?" Hank asked.

"During my time at college, I tried to belong to a college frat group. But for some unexplained reasons, I was rejected. Somebody said I was not smart enough. Others said my grades were not good enough. A few said I was a criminal who should be sent to prison. I decided to put a notice on Facebook, and found other students who were not allowed to join the same frat group, so we got together and decided to form our own special elite club. We made a pact, a code of honor, stating that, man for man, we would live together or we die together. Alfa coerced us to let him be our leader. He said he was a Greek scholar and he would select a good name for our club. He would use that knowledge to lead us forward. He knew all of us wanted some kind of revenge for not being accepted. We felt like social outcasts. So we tattooed our bodies and became a rebel underground group of rowdy people. Like gangsters, we packed a lot of heat. That heat is what got us in trouble."

Jack spoke up. "What kind of trouble?"

"We set fire to the frat club leader's car and had a sit-in in the dean's office. When he wouldn't listen to us, we put graffiti on his walls: profane Greek words. The newspapers lampooned us as misfits who deserved to be punished, but the cops had no proof.

"One night we were carousing in Mayfield's community campus, firing our guns in the air and at an empty water bottle lying on the ground, when a security guard came from out of nowhere, and tried to break us up. Alfa pointed his revolver at the man and, without hesitation, fired three shots at point-blank range. As the guard was lying on the ground, Alfa fired two more rounds."

"And you did nothing to help the security guard?" Hank was mad.

"As I already said, my fingerprints were on a cop's neck, and clothes. When things looked hopeless, and I knew I would be going to jail or the gas chamber, our leader, Alfa, suggested I should hide in his secret concrete cave until everything blew over. I thought that was really a cool thing to do. What a pal. Was I ever wrong?"

"Why didn't you tell the police who really did shoot the security guard?"

"I did. I was drunk on ouzo. Nobody believed me. My secret club said nothing to defend me. I know they were afraid of Alfa. They broke the club's creed to save their own necks."

"What about the weapon? Were there fingerprints on it?" "Alfa said he buried it but wouldn't say where."

Leonard was becoming somewhat unstable. "Rachel pleaded to go with me. Reluctantly, Alfa agreed. He blindfolded both of us and took us to some underground concrete cave, sorta like one of those bunkers in World War 11, that you see on TV. It was dusty and damp with no windows, but it did have an air vent in the roof. There was a single cot in the corner and a portable toilet nearby. A chest of drawers was on the opposite wall, and a small ice chest on top of it. From my prison time, I knew the area was about the size of a jail cell."

Hank started pushing ever harder for more answers. "How far away was this concrete cave?"

"I don't know, maybe five or ten miles out of town. I know we drove around a bit. Alfa gave Rachel and me some kind of pill. He said it would relax us. It sure did. It fogged up my mind real bad, but I do remember hearing a lot of trucks and cars whizzing by us at some point. My guess would be the concrete cave was, maybe, a few miles out of town on some nearby farmland. At night we could hear an owl calling for its mate. We listened for it every night. It helped us to keep our sanity, I do believe."

"How did you survive?" Hank asked.

"Slow down, Hank," Jack said. "Give the man time to respond. Remember what the nurse said."

"That's okay," Leonard nodded. "I want to get all this crap off my chest while I can. Every night, Alfa or one of our club members would deliver us a care package. Usually it consisted of a Styrofoam cup of soup, a sandwich, and an apple. If there was a full moon, I would laugh, and show Rachel the small label on the apple. The apple was from Brier's orchard. I use to play with their children many years ago."

Hank was adding up the score, so to speak. "So you want us to believe that you and Rachel lived in this concrete cave for seven years and that a member of your so-called club would bring you food each day, and take your crap, and your trash away."

"Yes, that's true. I am so sick of sandwiches I don't care if I never see another one in my life. I felt like a caged tiger and couldn't do anything about it."

Leonard started to slip off the deep end. His voice started to crack, and vile words poured forth. He let out a weird yell, said something in a language that neither Jack or Hank recognized, and rocked the bed violently.

Geri rushed into the room and jabbed the hypodermic needle into his thigh.

Leonard's upper body thrust upward, and then collapsed. "That sedative works fast," Jack said, amazed at its speed.

"Yes, it does. Without it, this man would not have lived. That is all the information you can get from him today. He will be out for quite a while. Maybe you can talk to him tomorrow afternoon, but don't count on it. Our lab downstairs is trying to find out what pills he was taking, that is, if he really was taking pills."

"What do you mean?"

"All his vital signs and brain scans read normal. Even his urine is clean. If he has been taking a drug for seven years, why doesn't it show up? I would say he is delusional, in a world of his own making."

Jack asked Geri. "I noticed two casts, one on each arm."

"Yes, when we did the preliminary testing, we found the right arm had been fractured years ago and was never reset. He couldn't move either arm and had no feelings in his fingers, so the doctors decided to break and reset both of them two days ago."

Jack looked at Hank. "Most people are right handed. David must have used his left hand to pull the trigger on that old revolver. No wonder he missed you."

"Ha. Ha. Too bad it wasn't you in the shed."

Jack winked at Geri. "Thanks for your help. We have to get back to the station. Hope to see you soon."

"Oh, you will. I am sure of that."

CHAPTER THIRTEEN

Joanna was walking up the steps from the newspaper basement carrying a heavy box of folders. She could see her boss, Charles Miller III, standing at the top of stairs. He was waiting to greet her with eyes of contempt. He was impolite and made no offer to take the box out of her hands, but, instead, fired a series of harsh demands at her. This was unusual behavior for Charles. Normally, he was not a slave driver; usually he was a calm, cool, collected kind of guy who ran a great newspaper, and treated his employees well.

But over the last two weeks he had become a real pain in one's neck. Joanna wanted to fire back with damaging insults or innuendos, but she thought better of it. She loved her new career and was determined to be the best in her field. This short, middle-aged, bald-headed man who stood in her way wasn't going to stop her. No way would she allow it to happen.

Charles's tenor voice reverberated off the walls beside her and ran down the basement steps. "Miss Selden, I know you're running late putting together the magazine for this weekend's edition. I will agree it's not an easy chore finding the history of this town. It's like some dark secret that someone doesn't want us to know. I have tried for years to find it myself, but I do know from my years in this business that you have a real nose for news. If anyone can find it, I know you will. So make no doubt about it.

Your report is due tomorrow if we are going to meet our deadline with the printers. Remember, I have given you one of the most important tasks researching the chronological history of Mayfield and, especially, the role the town played in the American Civil War. Again I repeat: if anybody can do it, I know it will be you."

Charles paused a few seconds and then lowered the boom on Joanna. "I don't know why, but the city council is putting extreme pressure on me to get this magazine ready. Maybe it has something to do with the election. Several members of the mayor's council I know are not so happy with the other candidate. Right now, they have my ass in a sling." He pointed his index finger at Joanna. "And yours could be there soon."Understand?"

Joanna had reached the top step and was just about fed up with the boss's demands. Her arms were aching from holding the heavy box. She hadn't eaten for hours, and she knew she needed to get to her work area soon or she might pass out. She acknowledged she understood the situation, brushed past her boss, and hurried down the hallway.

Her boss turned and watched her walk quickly away. "Oh, yeah, don't forget to do a good article about Joshua Jurvis too. They say he was the founder of our great town, Mayfield. I know that much. Without him our town would have never existed." Joanna listened to her boss's last statement with one ear, as she quickened her walking pace. She was determined to reach her desk.

Finally, when she saw she was close enough, she dropped the box on the edge of her desk, and plopped down on her cushioned chair seat. Beads of sweat formed on her forehead. She grabbed the tissue from her pants pocket and twice wiped her sweaty brow. Leaning back in her chair, she tried to relax and catch her breath. Joanna, at times, would glance at the box of folders. She envisioned it being a monolith trying to play tricks with her mind, like the one in Mr. Kubrick's space movie. It was warning her she should not begin to dig for the secrets it held, because she would be opening the lid to Pandora's box.

Screw it, Joanna thought. I am going to dig deep into you, bastard monolith, and find your heart, that is, if you have one.

Joanna thought for a moment about one thing the boss had said. She had to admit he was damn right. From the time she was a child, she had the uncanny ability of finding things other people missed. For example, she once found a woman's missing diamond ring in the cuff of a patrolman's pants. Now her intuitive mind was telling her she would find some new facts in these folders that would tie the history of Mayfield to the case Frank and Jack were working on. She also believed she was working on a bigger story than the history of Mayfield alone, and she wanted the exclusive rights to it.

Wiping her brow one more time, Joanna reached over, grabbed the box of folders, and started rummaging through it. She could see there were a lot of discolored papers and wrinkled news clippings in each folder topped with a fine layer of dust. She knew it would be a long and tedious process to uncover any important facts, but that was usually no bother to Joanna. She knew she could stay up all night for the following two days if she had to. She could control her sleep habits quite well. Forget the food, her gut feelings kept telling her to plow ahead with all gusto.

Joanna was deep into her work, and the hours slipped by fast. Only one person of the cleaning crew remained in the building on her floor. That person was mopping the end of the hallway when he heard a noise coming from the reporter's room.

Joanna had fumbled her bottled water and knocked it off the desk. It rolled over her feet, the last of the water spewing out and covering her Nikes. Having a mild hissy fit, she kicked the bottle under the desk and watched it roll across the floor.

In the process she happened to look up at the clock on the wall. Its large hands pointed to the twelve and the five. That's when Joanna realized it was early morning, and she had looked inside the box of folders umpteen times. She was so disappointed. She had found hardly anything of importance. She had sorted through all of the folders except for one and had found little of Mayfield's history. Most of the data in each folder consisted of a few obituaries, weather patterns, and minor civic meeting minutes. Nothing seemed newsworthy.

In kicking the water bottle, Joanna had also broken her concentration; she realized she was thirsty, tired, and disgruntled. In a final act, she reached for the last folder. *Forget forty-eight hours of work* , she told herself. It was about time to call it a night or morning. She looked at a water-stained green folder in her hand. All of the other folders were faded manila. She held the folder above her head and screamed. "Yes. Yes. There had better be something special in this green bastard."

After settling down, the first thing she spied was some cryptic writing on the outside flap. It looked like a code of some kind, such as somebody's email address. But she knew that couldn't be. The date on the tab was 1961. As a child, she had seen her mother use a typewriter to write letters. There were no email addresses back then. In fact, there were no personal computers either.

She pushed the box of folders farther aside, opened the green folder, laid it down on the desk, and proceeded to open it. Joanna knew her eyesight was getting blurry from the constant strain, but she forced herself to concentrate. The writing on the pages was very small and appeared to be almost unreadable. She noticed there were no typed words. Someone had used a fountain pen to create words so tiny that it forced Joanna to open her desk drawer and pull out a magnifying glass. What she was about to read would amaze her. She had found a treasure trove of historical information. She sensed it was very important and knew she would have to tell Jack and Frank soon. With the enthusiasm of a first grader, she continued to read with great excitement. She was oblivious to her surroundings.

Without warning, a black man stepped out of one of the darkened hallways and walked over to her desk. He looked down at a frightened Joanna. He sensed she had been deep in thought. A broad smile appeared on his face as he said in a gentle voice,

"Joanna, I hope I didn't scare you too much. I was almost finished with my cleaning when I heard a noise. Are you okay? I have finished my work, and I was leaving the building when I heard someone yelling."

The janitor's concern moved Joanna almost to tears. Something had broken Joanna's deep concentration once again, but this time she didn't care. Her brain had sucked out of the folder all the data that she needed. "Yes, Wally, I'm fine, and I'm getting ready to leave too." Joanna looked up and stared at the clock. It read 7:19 a.m. The time she had spent in the green folder had been well worth it.

"Okay, well, you have a good morning. Hope to see you tomorrow." "You have a nice day too."

Joanna was elated but felt cramps in her back and legs from sitting in one place for hours. She stood up and stretched her lithe body. Her search, she knew, was complete. Now she wanted to get to Jack and Frank as quickly as possible with the facts she had uncovered, and then she would grab the computer at home and author the articles she needed to meet the boss's demands. Maybe she thought she could get an assistant to help her. A smile appeared on her face. Her friend Patti might do it.

Grabbing the green folder and tucking it inside her coat, Joanna raced down the main hallway to the front lobby, rushed past some early morning employees streaming into work, and headed directly to her sports car.

In a flash she had the car burning rubber. Down Main Street she sped with her cell phone to her ear. She hoped her brother would be awake and in the police station. She was dying to tell him what she had uncovered.

Monday, November 2
6:23 a.m.

As Joanna Selden began steering her sports car off Broad Street, and into the Mayfield Police Station parking lot, she saw a silver Mercedes sedan rolling into a reserved parking space next to another silver Mercedes sedan. Both cars were close to the front door of the station. "Damn it," Joanna said, gritting her teeth. She knew who was behind the wheel of each Mercedes. The one already parked belonged to Samantha Jurvis, the female lawyer running for mayor. She liked to parade around, in showing off her luxury items, but Joanna wondered why she was here at this time of day?

The other sedan belonged to Chuck Hankin, Joanna's father, the police commissioner. *Why did he choose today to be an early riser?* Joan wondered. Because of his seniority on the police force, he prided himself on coming to work late, and, brazenly, telling everyone it was one of his earned perks. He wanted to make sure everyone knew who the boss was.

So what could be the reason for him coming to work so early? Joanna hoped there was no hanky panky going on between the two of them. Her father was old enough to be Samantha's father. Joanna was puzzled. She rationalized that, maybe, he couldn't sleep. He was a light sleeper. That seemed like a sound idea, so she decided to leave it at that for now.

Hoping her father didn't notice her, Joanna shifted the gear lever to reverse, backed up slowly, stopped, looked around, and then headed for the impound lot behind the police station building. She knew that the morning guard, Ted, should be on duty. He was a warm, friendly officer, and she knew that with just a little persuasion, he would allow her to park her sports car in the impound lot. Besides, Joanna always promised him she would stay only a few minutes, and she always kept her word.

But she still felt she had to keep, at least, two fingers crossed for good luck. Ted had to be there. She felt that the information she had stowed inside her coat needed to be delivered to Jack and Hank and nobody else.

Joanna knew she was taking a big risk by stealing a file from the newspaper office, and sneaking into the police station behind her father's back. She dreaded the abrasive language her father could spew out if he caught her in the cops' office. The bigoted commissioner simply could not, would not, accept her quitting the force and sinking so low as to work for a local newspaper. The working lineage of the family, he believed, was being a cop, or a housewife, and nothing else. He even tried to make her feel like an outcast to the entire family. *Poor Mom* , Joanna moaned, as she thought of having to put up with such a foul-mouthed man for all those years. How did she do it? What was her secret?

Luck was on Joanna's side. The gate to the impound lot was open. Joanna drove in and parked her car next to an old Honda Civic. She held up five fingers to Ted to indicate how long she would be. The handsome guard said nothing but smiled and pressed a button to open the rear door to the police station. Joanna raced through, and hurried up a single flight of steps. She stopped at the top to catch her breath. She could see Jack and Hank's office directly ahead.

As she walked closer, she observed that the office lights were on but no one was around. The office was empty and still. She did notice, though, the big bulletin board standing in the center of the office facing toward the front of each cop's desk. A plethora of newspaper clippings, photographs, and posits were attached to the board or strewn about their desks. *Don't they ever clean up their mess?* She thought. *How can anyone work like this? Ugh.*

Joanna panicked when she he heard the heavy footsteps of someone heading her way. *Thump. Thump.* Joanna quickly scanned the walls, looking for a place to hide. She soon realized she had only one place, and that was behind the bulletin board. She raced over and kept herself motionless, even holding her breath. She looked down and prayed no one would notice her fancy shoes sticking out from under the bottom of the board.

Thump. Thump.

Now a second person was coming her way. The second set of thumps sounded faster than the first. *Is someone trying to catch up to the first person?* Joanna thought.

Then nothing. No thumps at all.

"*Que pasa* , amigo, did you order a bulletin board with fancy shoes?" Joanna didn't recognize the stupid Mexican voice.

"*No* , El Capitan." Joanna failed to identify that voice either. She knew most of the workers in the building, but not these people. Who the hell were they, anyway?

"Pancho. Let's move it."

Joanna gave up and rushed out from behind the bulletin board. To her surprise she found herself facing Jack and Hank. They began roaring with intense laughter that was so hard they almost spilled their coffee. Joanna's face glowed red with embarrassment. She stopped and swung her fist at both of them. She missed their chins by inches while the folder stuffed in her coat fell to the floor.

"Okay, you smart-asses. Nice trick. You got me good. Really good. Just hope my father doesn't see us. I swear I'll lie and tell him you asked me to come in for a meeting. That'll do it. He hates me, but you two will really feel his wrath. You'll be laughing out of your own assholes."

Hank said, "How did you like our Mexican voices, senorita?"

A minute passed until all the laughter subsided. The three people stood in silence.

Joanna's face began losing some of its redness as she reached down to pick up the green folder. She raised it up in the air. "Okay, you have had your fun. In this folder are some interesting facts that should help your case."

She looked down the hallway. Various people were beginning to arrive at their desks.

"It's much too dangerous to be in here. Let's go down to the storage room, and I will show you what I found."

"Joanna," said Hank, "you know your father is in the building. And our future mayor is in his office."

"Yes, I know. He stays on this floor and never goes below to the storage room. We'll be safe there."

Once they reached the bottom floor, Jack unlocked the storage room and carefully opened the screened door. He flicked on the wall switch, and everyone stood around a table, eager to read the contents in the green folder.

Hank had to speak up. "Okay, Joanna, Just what have you brought in for us to see? And it had better be good."

"Well, Hank, I'm glad you asked." Joanna turned the folder on its side and pointed to the small writing. "See that, Hank and brother Jack? Do you know what those figures might be?"

Hank leaned in. "Looks like scribble to me." "No, Hank, you are wrong. Want to try again?" "No, let your brother try."

Jack made his guess. "Is it some kind of UFO writing? You know there has been several reports in this area." He smiled.

"No, what you see is the tiniest cursive writing that I have ever seen. It is in India ink, so it will last for centuries. I'd say it is the work of an educated young woman with a very steady hand. I had to use a high-powered magnifying glass to figure out what kind of writing it really was, and what it had to say."

"Okay, okay. Tell us what you have for us before someone comes down here and spoils our fun." Joanna could see Hank was nervous and already biting his fingernails.

Joanna held up an old, partly faded photograph. "Here it is, Hank. See this woman. She was the great-granddaughter of Joshua M. Jurvis. Her name is coded, but I was able to decipher it. She is Adeline May Jurvis. I looked for her name in all the files we have at the *Times Review* . There is no record of her name anywhere. She disappeared off the map."

"Maybe she is a ghost?" asked Jack, still smiling.

Joanna stared at Jack, and then she said, "For now, I'll call her Addie.""I believe Addie must have felt the history of the town was important, but for some unknown reason she didn't want anyone to know about it. In her secretive way, she wrote down that history and included some old news clippings and tarnished business papers."

"Okay, so who was she and what did she know that would help our case?"

Joanna looked into Hank's eyes. "Didn't your mother ever teach you manners?"

"Yeah, at the dinner table while we were eating roast beef, not history facts."

Joanna opened the folder and laid it out flat on the table. She pointed to an old sepia photograph. "That is Addie. In 1862 she wrote she was the teenage daughter of John Markum Jurvis, the mayor of Mayfield." Joanna paused. "Does that name mean anything to you? It should."

Both cops looked at each other, and then Jack spoke. "No, it does not. To my knowledge there is no family who lives in Mayfield today whose last name is Jarvis except our future mayor."

"That is right. But she is the person who changed their name several years ago, and you, Jack, knew her when you were a kid. Both played on the same little league baseball team I believe. What was her name then?"

"Samantha Bateman?" Jack replied.

Hank didn't quite buy the connection, or what Joanna was selling, but he was eager to learn more. "So what's in a name? There are probably dozens of Jurvise's living in the surrounding area, beyond Larksburg, or some who have moved farther away. Besides, that was two hundred years ago. The name proves nothing."

Joanna used her fingers to brush her hair back. "Damn you're good … usually, that is. Lizzie Bateman married a Jefferson Jurvis, and they had one child, Samantha Mae. Jefferson loved Lizzie, but his family did not. They said she wasn't good enough; she was an outsider. In despair, he committed suicide. But let me enlighten you further. Addie's story is quite interesting."

"She says she was sixteen years old, living in a trading post along Whiskey Creek. The Civil War was raging, and Union soldiers were running ammunition and supplies up to the front lines on the railroad tracks her grandfather had laid fifty years earlier."

"Addie says she heard cannon fire, and it sounded like it was getting closer instead of farther away. She was fearful the Confederates were advancing and her family must hide. Addie had collected notes on her great-grandfather and all his shady dealings. She kept them hidden in a green folder, which she hid under the floor of the wagon that would eventually move the family to a safer place.

"Addie removed the green folder from the wagon after the war was over and hid it under her bed. By the time she was twenty-one, she was working for the Mayfield Gazette, which eventually became the *Mayfield Times Review* newspaper. Her job was sorting and filing papers into boxes for the storage room. Addie knew she had found a safe place to keep her green folder."

"So Addie was a Jurvis who wrote about the Civil War," Hank said.

"Hold on! There is more. Lots more. "She married a fellow who was a distant cousin (same last name) who worked in a print shop. They had three children. The first son died from diphtheria at the age of six. The daughter became a seamstress and moved to Washington, D.C. She had the honor of making the first lady's gown for Chester Arthur's inaugural ball. The youngest son, Alfred M. Jurvis, became a very successful banker, but was despised by the townspeople. He charged exorbitant fees and ran a bootlegging business on the side. With the money he bought several acres of land on Castle Street in Mayfield, and built a large, gothic-looking home. He said he wanted that type of the home so he could scare the hell out of his neighbors' kids every day, not just on All Saint's Day. That's Halloween to you. He must have really hated children."

"Addie's original notes go on to paint her great-grandfather, Joshua, as an evil conniver, a tyrant. She wrote that prior to the Civil War he followed a wide stream (Whiskey Creek). It led him into a rugged piece of land surrounded by a ring of small green plateaus. He looked around and tested the ground. It was very acidic and pretty worthless for farming, but he had an idea. On a return visit he took his two sons and dug a tunnel more than fifty feet deep into the side of one of the surrounding plateaus. They melted down pieces of silver coins he had saved, and placed the tiny, hard pieces in the roof of the cave. His sons went back to the town, and started spreading the news that silver had been found in the lower Mayfield County. The father already had bought up a lot of that land, erected a trading post and started selling bogus land rights. He made a fortune.

"He even put in the railroad to entice all the local commoners to take a look-see. Unfortunately, the father drank some bad rotgut whiskey from a close neighbor, and he died suddenly. The family, though grief stricken, decided to stay put. They were all money mongers. They felt there was still a fortune to be made right here in Mayfield."

"I might also add that Joshua and his sons were strict abolitionists. He used his railroad tracks as avenues to move slaves to safer grounds. But first he would keep them in his so- called silver mine and charge them a fee. He made thousands of dollars profiteering off them until the war ended. He became a very wealthy man and the real start of the Jurvis Empire."

"Wonderful story but what does it tell us?" Jack asked.

"There's more. Someone added information in 1923. The person did not give his name, but I can tell it is a man's handwriting. I also wondered how he found the green folder. Was he a reporter? We'll probably never know."

"What did he have to say?" Hank asked. "That person, whoever he was, found a few pages of a ledger that showed someone named Thomas M. Jurvis was following in her grandfather's footsteps. He was making moonshine and selling it to two speakeasies on

Broad Street and Clearwater Street right here in Mayfield. This Jurvis character also had a brother who was arrested for killing a rival gang member, but was never prosecuted. Not nice people in the Jarvis family empire, I'd say."

Joanna added her personal take on the subject. "So, you see, corruption might be a hereditary factor in the Jurvis family. I would bet that the Jurvise's today have a few skeletons in their closet that they don't want anybody to know about."

Jack spoke with firmness. "Joanna, this is all supposition. You know that. It wouldn't hold up in court at all. You can't arrest someone on bad ancestry or your gut feelings."

"Jack, you're right, but haven't I proven the Jurvis family has remained a hidden force in Mayfield all these years? And nobody knows about it. Jack, years ago our father used to play golf each week with Andrew Davis, our dentist and close neighbor. He told our father in strict confidence that he knew the Jurvis family quite well. He said they kept a very low profile to draw no attention, much like the Masons do. I tell you, someone is pushing me extra hard for the town's history. Isn't it strange a lot of evidence has already come to you, and you have no real suspects? Why? I will tell you. Something major is about to happen in Mayfield. I can feel it, and I mean really soon. I believe the Jurvis family will, turn out, to be a big part of it."

"Okay," Jack said. "You made your point. Let's leave it at that for now." He paused. "I am curious about one thing. How did Mayfield get its name. I have heard many rumors. Does this Addie tell us anything "Joshua loved his wife so much that he decided to name the town in her honor by using her maiden name.

Thump. Thump.

Somebody was coming down the steps. Joanna prayed it wasn't her father. "Miss Selden, I thought you said you would be only a few minutes. We need the car space. They're bringing in a wreck right now."

Joanna and both cops were relieved. "Ted, I am so sorry. We were discussing some important things, and time just got away. How did you find us?"

"I know you spend a lot of time down here, so I took a chance."

"Please don't tell anyone."

"Yes, madam." The cop touched his hat and started to walk up the steps. Joanna closed the green folder, and she, and Hank and Jack followed the guard outside.

That's when Hank's eagle eye spotted the tow truck dumping off a wreck, a black pickup truck. The front end was smashed in. Bloodstains had been spattered around the cracked windshield, side door, and quarter panel.

"Jack, that's the truck we saw the other day. Robert Sandoz had stopped it for speeding near the judge's house."

"You're right. That is the truck. I wonder what happened."

Jack and Hank walked over to a fat man who wore no belt and had the crack in his ass showing above his dirty underwear. He was walking between the tow truck and the wrecked pickup, trying to unhitch the tow cables.

"Hi. My name is Jack, and this is my partner, Hank. What can you tell us about this wreck?"

The man looked at the two cops and wiped his forehead with an oily rag. "Hi. All I can tell you is we got a call to come to Ashford Road. There had been a bad accident. The guy driving this pickup apparently lost control of the vehicle and hit a group of trees. The emergency team arrived, but it was too late. The man was terribly bruised and had lost a lot of blood. The coroner pronounced him dead at the scene. When I came to the scene, the EMTs were loading the body into the ambulance."

Jack asked. "By chance, did you see the body, maybe the arms?"

"No, I didn't but I did hear one of the EMTs mention what he thought was an ugly tattoo. He said it looked like a diamond with the letters *"AL "* inside it."

"Thanks for the information. We might want to talk to you at a later date."

The man released the cables, climbed back into the cab, nodded to the cops, and drove away.

"Just another piece of the puzzle." Jack was calm as he pulled his cell phone out of his pocket. "Dan, Hank and I are at the impound yard. Get the CSI team down here to the impound lot right away. I want the team to go over a black pickup truck with a fine-tooth comb. It is really important. Its license plate reads "A-L-F-A-1." Do a complete examination. Thanks."

"Yeah, Jack," said Hank. "I agree with an earlier statement you made." "What's that?"

"I am getting tired of counting pieces and not finding any of them fitting together."

Back in their office, Jack stood in silence while Hank added Joanna's information to the bulletin board. When Hank was about finished, Jack stepped forward and started to peer over Hank's shoulder. He knew Hank had a knack for arranging all the various pieces of evidence in the order he thought was most correct. Jack had always liked Hank's approach to sorting out clues, and aiding his police friends in finding the guilty person, or persons. But he was not good at being the leader in a search; that type of responsibility was too much for him.

Hank felt Jack's breath. "You got my back?" he asked jokingly.

"That's a big back to cover, Ollie." Jack replied. He took two steps to the left side of Hank to get a better view of all the evidence, his eyes always searching for any plausible answers that might help solve the case. "What the hell is going on here? he thought aloud. "Why can't I find the common thread that ties all this together?

At one point he raised his hand and held his chin, much like the old-time comedian Jack Benny would have done. Then, realizing Hank might be wrong, Jack began focusing his eyes on each trivial fact, delving deeper and deeper into thought, trying to rearrange the pieces of evidence to fit the puzzle as he saw it.

Hank was a little perturbed at Jack's silence, but he knew better than to disturb him. This was Jack's quiet time. Hank had learned from past experiences, that Jack, possessing a high degree of intelligence matched with a superior memory recall system, needed time to concentrate his thoughts. With amazing accuracy, Jack could usually find that common thread.

Hank could also see Jack had been getting unnerved of late and was growing irritable with his inability to crack the case. On occasion when Hank would glance at his partner, he could almost believe that the harder Jack tried to solve the puzzle, the farther he was from finding the answers.

A long period of silence prevailed, except for the sound of the clock on the wall. Then Jack's cell phone rang. It rang again, and again. Jack was a silent sentinel, oblivious to everything.

An agitated Hank turned his back to the bulletin board and broke the silence with a loud demand. "Will you answer your damn cell phone?"

Jack, his trance now broken, pulled the phone out of his shirt pocket, and answered the call in a rather nonchalant voice. "Hello, Jack Hankin speaking."

"You have a rather soft voice today. Is everything okay?" It was Geri, the nurse at the hospital.

A small smile developed on Jack's face. "Yes, I am fine. What's up?"

"I am taking an unscheduled coffee break, and I am sitting at corner table at Sloan's Luncheonette on Main Street. I have some information you might like to know."

"What is it? And, by the way, it has been a while since David had his relapse. How is he doing now? When can we talk to him?"

"Hold on, Jack. You are getting as jumpy as your partner; please, one question at a time."

"I'm sorry. Forgive my impatience?"

"I forgive you. Now, the reason I am calling you from here is because thatI thought you should have the information before the news gets out, especially to that sister of yours."

Jack knew Geri and Joanna didn't see eye to eye on things, especially since Joanna had questioned Geri's competence during a recent court hearing. "What news?"

"Leonard Anders died this morning."

"What? It can't be. He is our star witness. That son-of a-bitch." Jack threw his hands up in despair. "What's going on?"

Hank stared at his partner, his mouth open.

Geri had to raise the volume in her cell phone. "Calm down, Jack. Are you still there?"

Jack's outbreak subsided as quickly as it had arisen. He regained his composure, and placed the phone next to his ear.

"Again, I'm sorry. Forgive me. We're under a lot of pressure here at the station. Please tell me what happened."

"Last night Leonard's skin started turning a whitish color. I mean, it soon became pure white. It was scary even for me. I had never seen that happen before. I've seen jaundice turn people's skin yellow, but nothing that turns people white. He looked like a skinny ghost made up for Halloween. The cop who was on duty called me, and we stayed with Leonard all night until he died early this morning. That is the same time our lab had finally figured out what the substances were in his body, but it was too late to save him." "Substances?"

"Yes, Jack, someone had given him a cocktail mix of *Ageratina Altissima* laced with heroin by-product a day or two before he was admitted to the hospital."

"And just what is Ageratina Altissima?"

Geri's voice dropped a little, but she felt duty bound to give a complete answer. "*Agertina Altissima* is a plant that is called White Snakeroot, and it contains a poison, tremetol, which destroys the human body in sixty to ninety hours. The disease is more commonly known as "Milk Sickness.""

"Milk Sickness? Where does this plant grow?"

"White Snakeroot is a wild plant that cows sometime eat, and it gets into their milk. It usually grows in the autumn and is found in meadows along the edges of forests."

"Doesn't it kill the cow first?"

"No, it doesn't hurt the cow, but it will destroy any person who ingests the milk. In a short time, the victum's body turns milky white. Vomiting and convulsions follow, and finally respiratory failure occurs. Abraham Lincoln lost his mother to this strange disease."

"Why doesn't the public get this disease today?"

"The milk industry has placed tight controls on all milk and its by products for years. Pasteurization, blending milk from various dairies, and things like that."

"I see."

Jack's thoughts returned to the deceased man. "I'm so sorry to hear about Leonard. He seemed like an unlucky man who happened to get caught in a very bad situation, one that he could not get out of."

"Yes, I agree. His body also showed signs of beatings, severe malnutrition, and anemia."

"By chance, did Leonard say anything before he died?"

"That's another reason I called you. Sometime around one a.m. the cop outside his room heard Leonard tossing about in his bed. At that time Leonard's skin was just starting to turn whitish. So he called me. I raced to his room and found Leonard trying to vomit, but nothing was coming out. I gave him a sedative to calm him down, and that's when he started babbling on about his life inside a concrete cave."

"Wait a second, Geri, I want Hank to hear this too." Jack motioned to Hank to listen up as he switched his cell phone to speaker mode. "Okay, please continue. What did Leonard have to say?"

"I couldn't tell if Leonard was delusional, but this is part of what he told us. The rest of his babbling I was able to record on my cell phone, and I will be sending that to you after we finish our conversation." "Okay?"

"That will be fine."

"Leonard said he was one member of a very secretive club. Alfa, a tall, muscular man, who said he liked reading the memoirs of Socrates, Aristotle, and Karl Marx, coerced all of the members to choose him as their leader. He convinced all the club members he could lead them in the fight to do away social injustice, and have true democracy like the ancient Greeks had. We soon found out he cared little about ancient writings or injustice. He wanted to be a tyrant. Nothing could be done to stop him, because the treasurer and backer of the club supported him. Alfa was a plain hooligan with a hidden temper, and an evil one at that."

"Go on, Geri. What else did he say?" Geri took a sip of her coffee.

Leonard told us a story about Alfa's preteen life. He said that when Alfa and his buddy, Jason Riggs, were kids, they liked to go fishing in Whiskey Creek. One summer morning they made fishing poles out of weeping willow branches and were having a lot of fun trying to catch the hungry trout swimming in the rain-swollen waters. But they soon lost track of time. To make it home and not face the wrath of their mothers, they decided to avoid the slow, marshy trail, and take a shortcut that ran along the shoulder of Highway 11A."

Geri looked out the front window. She saw a group of people exiting a tour bus.

"Sorry, but there is a large group of people getting off a bus, and they are coming in here. I'll have to end my coffee break now, but I am going to send you the rest of what Leonard said." "Goodbye" Geri dropped a five dollar bill on the table, and hurried out the door.

Jack looked first at the cell phone, and then at Hank. "Did you hear all of that conversation?" Hank nodded. "Hank, I think I am starting to see the beginning of the thread."

"Good thing. I was getting worried about your deep concentration. That's the worst I have ever seen it. I wondered if you were going to make our bulletin board levitate."

"Maybe I'll do it for you next time."

The indicator light went on. Jack's cell phone began blinking, alerting him that he had received the text. "Come closer, Hank, so we both can hear what Leonard's last words were."

Jack pressed the play icon and laid the cell phone on his desk. Leonard's scratchy voice came on, loud and clear. He was describing the events that had taken place between Alfa, Jason, and Rachel.

"Alfa and Jason were running along the shoulder of Highway 11A when Jason spied a dark object ahead. As they got closer, they could see it was a hole of some kind that was partially covered with weeds, and debris. They assumed the heavy rains that had fallen the night before must have made the hole. Jason pointed it out to Alfa, and both of them decided to stop and investigate.

"It was a rather small hole, maybe a foot and a half wide, barely visible to the passerby. It reminded Jason of a culvert on the side of a road in front of his house. Sometimes, in the spring, wildflowers would shoot up nearby.

"They peered down into a dark abyss. It looked scary. Jason dared Alfa to shimmy through the hole, and see what was below. Alfa accepted the challenge. When he touched bottom, he yelled for Jason to follow.

"Once inside, they could see it was like a room made of concrete walls with strange writings and symbols carved into them. In the back of the room was a mass of dirt and rubble blocking any other exits? In one corner was a small table with a pile of bedding resting on it. Jason and Alfa looked at each other, and they both felt fear, wondering what kind of creature lived there. Both of them turned around and fought each other to make a rapid climb out of the concrete room. As they exited the hole, they came face-to-face with a very large black man. He was a mountain of a man holding a brown bag in one hand and a pitchfork in the other. Both of them were awestruck by his huge presence and just wanted to run, that is, until the man spoke.

"In a deep but kind voice he said, "Well, looks like you, youngins, found my home." As he raised the brown bag, the man could see Jason and Alfa were still afraid. "Let me introduce myself. My name is Fred, Fred Brown, and this is my dinner. It is fried chicken and biscuits my nanny made me an hour ago."

Fred pointed to the hole in the ground. "Please come down and join me."

"Alfa tried to not accept the invitation. "We can't stay. Our mothers are fixing dinners for us."

"Can't you stay just a short while?"

Not sure of the consequences if they tried to escape, Jason and Alfa agreed, shimmied down the hole for a second time, and sat on the concrete floor. Fred threw the pitchfork into some tall brush. Although he was a large man, he could shimmy with the best of them.

"Once seated, Fred opened the bag and pulled out a quart of soda pop. Then he handed to each of the others a fried chicken leg, a buttermilk biscuit, and a napkin.

"I have to keep this place clean. When you are finished, put all the trash in the bag." After taking a bite, Jason looked at Alfa and smiled. The chicken was delightful.

"Fred took a swig of the soda pop and passed it around. Alfa's curiosity was piqued. He had to find out more about this black man. "Fred, why do you live here and not with your nanny?"

"Fred wiped his mouth with a napkin. "First, you tell me your names." "Most people call me "Alfa," and this is my best pal, Jason."

"And why do they call you Alfa?"

"Alfa frowned. "Because my parents are from Greece and I was their first child."

Fred understood. "Nice names for two young boys. Now, Alfa, I will answer your question. You are sitting in a secret room that use to hide black people like me, who were trying to escape slavery in the south.""Did you know there was slavery in this country about one hundred and fifty years ago?"

A demure Jason spoke "Yes, Alfa and I read about it in our history class last year."

"Well, this room was a place where the black people could hide temporarily on their escape to the north and freedom." Fred pointed toward the back of the room. "See that pile of dirt and rubble? I was told there used to be an exit door before the highway builders came along and tried to fill this room in. By luck, they missed getting all of the room."

"Was this part of the Underground Railroad?" Alfa asked.

"That's right." Fred looked amazed. "If the slaves made it this far, a kind family named Bateman that lived in the house across the field, had food and clothing waiting for them in this concrete room. Then, on the next night, the owner of that house would lead them across the field to a secret cellar door. He led them through a coal bin and upstairs, where the missus would encourage them with Bible teachings, and send them on their way. I believe my nanny's great-great-grandmother was one of those people who found freedom this way."

"Did the owner make this room all by himself?"

"Not exactly. You see, years ago, before the Underground Railroad, some white people came here and pretended to dig a silver mine. Nanny told me they were bad white people because they planted bits of silver in the mine to trick the local people into buying property. They told the local people they could make a fortune. The silver mine turned out to be a complete bust. The only ones who became rich were the bad white people who had sold the land to them. They eventually took complete control of Mayfield County."

Alfa had another question. "I thought miners used wood instead of concrete to support the walls and roof of a mine?"

Abel looked at him. "Alfa, my son, you are a very smart boy. You are right, and if we would scrape some of this concrete away, you would find that those pieces of wood are still there. You see, the Batemans, who saved our people, cemented the front portion of the mine so they would have a warm and dry place to stay."

"Wow. What a story. This will be my next paper for English class." Jason paused. "If that's okay with you, Fred?"

"Sure is okay with me."

"So why do you want to live here?" asked Jason.

"I wanted to pay my respects to all the black people who suffered here. But I couldn't come close to this place for years without being shot at. Someone with a high-powered rifle, was living in a large house on the other side of the highway. That person had me in his sights anytime I came too close. One bullet ripped into the toe of my boot. Lucky for me the steel tip in the boot stopped it, or else I would be missing a few toes."

"Why do you come here now? Aren't you afraid someone will try to shoot you?"

"One day that large house caught fire. I could see the smoke billowing high in the sky, and hear the fire engines too. After that, there were no more bullets whizzing by and burying themselves in the dirt. I think the person with the rifle must have lost his house for good."

"I climbed down the hole and found this orange crate and some old bedding, so I stayed." Fred pointed to the wall. "See those names and dates scratched in the walls? My relatives wanted me to remember them, and so I do, just about every day."

"Jason poked Alfa in the side. He knew Jason was telling him it was time to go.

"Alfa smiled at Fred as he handed the brown bag back to him. "We are really late for dinner. We have to go now. Thanks for the chicken leg and biscuit."

"You are most welcome, and please come again. I'll tell you some stories that my nanny told me about Uncle Remus."

"Alfa looked at Jason. Both wondered who in the world Uncle Remus was. Fred helped boost both of them through the hole. Alfa noticed when Fred stood up, that half his body was above the ground. He watched them walk away and waved good-bye. Alfa looked back one last time and pointed to the pitchfork.

"No, leave it there, said Fred. "I will need it in the morning to bail hay for the neighbor down the road."

"Alfa smiled and raced to catch up with Jason, who was walking fast to get home."

Suddenly Leonard started shaking and went through a bad coughing spell, then he settled down, and began to speak again.

"The reason I have told you that story is Jason told me Alfa visited Fred a few more times over the years, and grew to admire him very much. Sadly, Fred died from pneumonia, but Alfa always made it a point to pay a visit to that concrete room. My mistake was allowing Alfa to tell Rachel and I about it. He thought it would be a good place to hide until all the hoopla about the security guard's murder had died down. Rachel and I agreed. But that bastard turned out to be a jail keeper and ruined both our lives"

"I loved Rachel, and it was a damn sin to keep her trapped in that concrete room for seven years. She became more and more paranoid as the time went by. Finally, Rachel told me she had had enough and was getting out of this hellhole. She didn't know her father was nearby, searching for her.

"Rachel, Rachel. This is your father. Where are you? Jaspar found your handkerchief.He is here with me. We know you are around here somewhere." "It was her father's voice. Rachel grew excited, and yelled as loudly as she could. "Daddy, I am over here near the highway. Please help me!" In her excitement she forgot someone had a rifle aimed at us twenty-four hours a day. I wanted to stop her, but it was no use. She pushed me over the table, and stuck her head up out of the hole. A high-powered bullet pierced her skull, and she fell back into my arms. She died instantly. I had no chance to say good-bye. I started to sob. I had lost my one true love. Why? For a killing I didn't do."

"Then I heard footsteps coming closer and heard a human voice. I knew it must be the judge. I could hear the person walk closer but stop a foot away. I could hear the dog barking. Then I heard some more footsteps.

"So you're the son-of-a-bitch who has my daughter, not Leonard." The judge clenched the handle of his revolver even harder.

"'Yes, that's right, big man. It's me, Alfa, or as you know me in the courtroom, Edwin Caste. You, the tall and mighty judge who sends people like my old man to prison."

"Your old man?"

"Shut up. I said enough. Take a step back and see your daughter. She is in the hole right behind you."

"The judge did take that step while keeping a close eye on Alfa "Rachel, are you there? It's your father."

"I saw a bullet from across the highway pierce the judge's left ankle. Pieces of bone flew everywhere. A brief exchange of words followed, and then I heard three shots fired all at once. I heard the judge's body hit the ground hard, and it covered some of the hole. I find it strange that no more bullets were fired from across the highway. I assume Alfa had some way of controlling that, like a remote button.

"Seconds later, Alfa pushed the body aside, and poked his face into the hole. His face was red, and the arteries in his neck were bulging. He was very irate.

"Now you don't have to worry about her family any more," he said. "They're all gone."

"Alfa stared at the bloodstains around the hole. That's when I saw an axe in his right hand. He told me he always parked his truck in front of the hole and kept an axe, a blanket, and a rifle under the seat of his truck just for good hunting, and today was one of his good days."

"Alfa stretched his left hand down the hole, and grabbed Rachel's head by the hair. I was too weak to fight back. He pulled her head just above the surface of the highway and swung the axe in a giant arc. Acting like Hercules on Mount Olympus, Alfa raised her head in triumph. If that wasn't enough, he placed the head down on the ground and swung the axe again, chopping into two halves. One half he threw down the hole and into my face. He kept the other half. He wrapped it in a red scarf, and, I believe, laid it on the front seat of his truck. He looked down the hole and yelled that his half was for the judge. The judge wanted Rachel home, so Alfa was granting his final wish. Alfa yelled in my face, saying that the judge was the bastard who had tried to ruin our little club and that it was his damn dog that had found my hiding place. "They deserve the daughter's head, he said so I will drop it in his mailbox. With little effort, Alfa flexed his biceps and heaved the judge's body into the truck bed. Next, he reached down the hole, grabbed Rachel's body, and heaved her into the truck bed as well."

On the recorder, Jack and Hank could hear Geri ask Leonard a question. "Leonard, how did you wind up in this condition?"

"When I heard Alfa get into his truck and drive away, I decided I wanted to give Rachel's skull a proper burial and tell my story to the police. Alfa is a very dangerous person who needs to be put in the gas chamber before he kills somebody else. I feared Alfa would return and throw me in some dump like he said he did with the others. Remembering what Fred had said about another exit covered by the dirt and rubble, I grabbed the large tin can that I had to pee in each day, and began clearing a tunnel. I had renewed vigor because I had a purpose in life, and I was determined to fulfill it." "Working as hard as I could, I was able to burrow, maybe, eight feet into the damp soil and stone before I felt something hard above my head. It was round and the size of a manhole cover. Using both my feet, I was able to pry it up and free it from six inches of soil and the tangled roots of wild ivy. I shimmied through the opening carrying Rachel's skull with me."

"It was a moonlit night, so I had to creep across the damp fields on my hands and knees. I had Rachel's skull dangling under my chin, her hair in my mouth. Even if I had wanted to, I don't think I could have stood up after being kept in that cave for seven years."

"I found the back of Lizzie Bateman's house, just like Fred had told Alfa and Jason. I felt along the wall and touched a small gap. I just knew it had to be the end of the removable panel. I squeezed my fingers between the gap and the wall and pulled as hard as I could. The removable panel gave way and allowed me to reach the coal bin. Inside the basement, I turned the dampers on the furnace, and stoked the fire. I got it good and hot. I was afraid Alfa's dog would find the skull if I buried it, so that's why I decided to cremate a part of her. I remember Rachel had become so thin and frail that her skin barely covered her skull. I said a prayer and pushed her skull into the furnace. Her long black hair followed and burned brightly for a few seconds. I grabbed the poker leaning against the furnace, and pushed the skull to the back."

"I heard a noise outside. Alfa had found me. He was yelling at his dog to go back to the truck. Seconds later, I saw him emerge from the coal bin carrying an axe. Right then I thought he was going to cut me up into pieces. Instead, Alfa punched me again and again until I couldn't move. He dragged me back through the coal bin and to the outdoor shed. He smashed the lock on the shed door with his axe, and threw my limp body inside. I could barely hear Alfa race across the field to get his truck, which he must have left at the "…""

There was a lot of commotion in Leonard's hospital room. Jack and Hank could hear people moving around, some yelling out orders. There were items being moved and lifted about. At that point Jack and Hank could hear Leonard having a series of convulsions. Then silence.

Geri's voice came from the recorder. "Leonard Anders has died."

The recorder continued to run, but there were no more voices or sounds. Jack pressed the stop button. Both cops stood in silence for a few moments. They knew life had a beginning and an end. The beginning was a joy. In their line of work, the end usually meant deep sorrow.

Jack spoke. "I didn't even have time to thank Geri. Her help has been invaluable."

"Now we have a big piece of the puzzle, Jack. You can ease up on all that thinking you've been doing of late."

"Yes, but one part of the puzzle is still messing. I believe there is a big prize to be won, and who is the one that wants to win it? Why me, ofcourse."

"Quit the bullshit, Stan. We still have to go to the Larksburg dumps."

CHAPTER SIXTEEN

Stepping on the piles of floating garbage in a remote part of the Larksburg dump reminded Jack of walking on his grandmother's waterbed, except this one was covered in a putrid layer of decayed vegetable and fecal matter. A terrible smell escaped with each sinking footstep he took. And that is how Jack described it to dump employee, Will Tiller. Will, a young towhead, operated a front- end loader, and he had agreed to lead the two men, along with the dump owner, to the remotest part of the Larksburg dumping grounds. The report Jack had received from the Larksburg Police indicated that two or more bodies had been discovered at this dumpsite. Jack's gut instinct told him that the names of these bodies would be of the utmost importance in solving the case Hank and he were trying to solve.

Hank and the owner of the dump followed close behind Will and Jack while trying to maintain their balance. Hank was not a gifted athlete, so he studied Jack's steps and tried his best to place his boots in each of Jack's boot prints before they disappeared beneath the surface. He wrinkled his nose when detecting the nauseating smells of gases oozing up from all the decay, and to him it smelled terrible, like rotten eggs. He prayed silently he did not fall into any of that crap. He did not want to face the stern looks his wife would make when he arrived home smelling like a privy. That thought bothered him a lot. She might throw the spaghetti pot at him this time. *Boy, would that do some damage*, he thought. Might even destroy the few hairs I still have left on my head.

Will moved a step ahead of the rest, and then stopped in front of his front- end loader. "This is how far I was able to drive my loader. Now it is stuck in this fuckin' shit. And it is going to take a lot to pull it out."

He pointed ahead to a huge pile of garbage emitting a myriad of ungodly smells.

"That's what my loader pushed before it got stuck."

Will informed them he had walked around this part of the dump the previous morning to assess its condition. He thought he saw part of an arm sticking out of the blackened garbage, so he reported it to the owner. The owner looked came by and saw nothing but reported it to the Larksburg Police anyway.

Now the piled-up garbage looked like a huge black wave. The two cops and the dump owner could see how badly Will's loader was stuck. The blackened garbage had risen two feet on each side of it. No way was Will going to drive his loader out of this quagmire. Past experience had taught Will he would need a heavy-duty tow truck with a very long winch to pull it out. And he knew had better be soon or else he would have no loader at all. The acid in the garbage was already starting to take the paint off the track ways.

Will pointed to the deep trough that now existed in front of his loader. Ten feet in front of that, they saw the black pile Will's loader had created. It was a huge mass of crap that didn't seem to move. "When I made that is when I first saw the bodies. As it grew in size, I saw some big objects rise upward just beneath the surface. At first I couldn't tell what they were. They were all covered in that black shit. Then, as I was able to back up a few feet, a black pole rose up above the surface and then sank back down under that huge pile of garbage. I couldn't move my loader after that, but I saw what looked like fingers on the end of that pole. By its shape, I knew that I had seen an arm, not a pole."

Next Will pointed to another smaller blob of black garbage partly hidden behind the far end of the pile. It seemed to be moving or growing in size. "Over there you can see the coroner."

"Coroner?"

"Yes, he is bending over, looking for more bones."

At the sound of Will's voice, the coroner stood up. He was covered from head to toe in the black garbage.

Will waved as he said. "He was here last evening and has been here all this morning as well. Jack waved too. "I am Jack Hankin of the Mayfield Police Department. We will be over to see you in a minute. You can fill us in on what you found."

The coroner did not wait to talk but nodded in approval and waved his gooey, blackened arm. Then he returned to probing around in the garbage once again, looking for more body parts.

Jack and Hank peered into the black abyss that was in front of them. Hank spoke first, as usual. "What is this smelly mess?"

Will replied, "There is a black liquid as thick as tar that oozes out of the ground on different occasions. It mixes with all the animal and vegetable matter. Nothing can live in it. I never wanted to come to this part of the dump, because my loader always gets stuck in this shit, and I wined up losing a day's pay."

"So why did you decide to try now?" Jack asked.

Will's boss volunteered to answer that question. "The dump is getting quite full, and the local authorities say we must find more space or we will face stronger EPA restrictions. They are so stringent we would have to move. Finding another site would take at least two years. That would cost the taxpayers of Larksburg and Mayfield a lot of money. I told Will to try to clear this area. I agreed to pay him a day's wages even if he failed."

Hank replied. "It looks like he failed to me. My feet are sinking into this stuff as we stand around talking."

"Don't worry. I have a large sheet of plywood. You can stand on that." Will walked to the back of the loader and pulled it off the top of the engine cowling. He laid it down before Hank's feet. Hank was glad to step on something solid that wouldn't move much. He had made up his mind. He didn't want to go any farther. He would let Jack collect all the evidence he could find in this smelly cesspool.

Jack asked a few more minor questions as he and Will started to plow their way through the trough and toward the coroner. He turned his head toward Hank. "Are you coming?"

Hank looked around. He shook his head. He wanted no part in this next scene. "No, I am going back to the dump's office. I'll snoop around there. Maybe I can find some clues. I'll see you later."

Jack and Will kept on trudging forward while Hank and Will's boss tried to make a hasty retreat.

Jack came up to the coroner, who was bent over, and tapped him on the back.

"Coroner, if you did not hear me, my name is Detective Jack Hankin of the Mayfield Police Department. We were informed there were dead bodies or body parts found here. Can you confirm that?"

"Yes, there are many."

The coroner rose and looked Jack squarely in the eye. He stood there looking like theHulk covered in black sludge. "Jack, My name is Ken Nolan. I'd shake your hand if mine were not so dirty. I am the coroner for both counties. What a wonderful job I have. I think our state government is trying to save money by having only one coroner for two counties, and that's me. Glad to meet you."

"I have been here for fourteen hours or so, and I have found three bodies so far. I think there could be more buried in this awful garbage. By the way, don't let any of this stuff touch your skin. It is highly infectious and dangerous to your system. That's why I am wearing a diver's suit to protect me from all this muck."

"What have you found so far? Are the bodies male or female?"

Ken reached down in the muck and raised a slender arm. "This one is a female. She was probably thirty years old, I would guess. But it is hard to really tell because she is missing her head. That seems unusual, since bones in this garbage are preserved quite well. This place reminds me of the fossilized bones I found at La Brea Tar Pits in Los Angeles last summer. I can't imagine what could have happened to this woman's head."

"Are there any distinguishing marks or tattoos on the body?"

"No, I checked all over but couldn't find any. No scars or other identifying features." Ken moved toward another spot. "Here we have two men, each one about five feet eight inches tall." He lifted up another arm. "This man was shot once in the heart, and he has gray hair. No distinguishing marks, either. He was clutching a handkerchief in his left hand. I cannot make out anything unusual about it. Most of the handkerchief has started to rot away."

Jack thought for sure this must be the judge's body. "Can I have that handkerchief for a while?"

"Sure, if it helps you. Just send it back to the Larksburg Police Department when you finish with it."

"Can you say how long they have been here?"

"It is really hard to tell for sure, but my guess is no more than a few days, maybe a week at the very most. The acid in this dump eats the flesh away pretty fast."

"Where is the other body you found?"

The coroner dropped the arm, reached deeper into the garbage, and pulled up another arm. "This short man had one bullet hole that went through his back and into his heart."

"Any distinguishing features on him?"

"He has wavy black hair." Ken scraped the garbage off the arm. "This arm has a tattoo of a diamond with legs, I guess, and the letters "*PH*" inside the diamond."

"Anything else?"

"No, not so far, but I am still searching."

"Thanks for the information. Call me if you do find anything else. I have left my phone number in the office."

"I am waiting for the tow truck with a net attached to a cable. These bodies are impossible to move any other way. Maybe I will have more information for you then."

Jack and Will turned and started the long trek back to the office.

Ken walked a few steps farther away and started probing again. This time he had to reach even deeper, and the smelly garbage almost touched his chin. His hand touched something. He grabbed a hold of what was possibly, a tree limb, and yanked hard to raise it up. "Jack!" he yelled. "I have the arm of another body. Come back."

Jack and Will turned around and headed back to Ken. "We'll be there in a minute. Hold on."

Ken was holding the arm up in the air and trying to wipe off some of the garbage when Jack and Will returned.

"By chance do you see any distinguishing marks or tattoos on this body?" Jack asked.

"At first there seems to be none. However, when I rolled the body over, I could see she had the word "Alfa" tattooed on her shoulder.

"She?"

"Yes, it's a female, maybe thirty years old, I would guess. And you can see she is missing an arm."

"Well, thanks again." The stench was starting to get to Jack. He was beginning to feel nauseated and knew he had to get back to the dump's office soon.

Jack and Will started out once again to return to the office. The garbage in certain places was deeper than in other places, and it rose above their knees as they traveled.

Both of them were as smelly as skunks when they finally reached the office door. Hank opened the door and greeted them before they could enter. He directed them to an outdoor shower area, and told them to throw their dirty clothes in a special box. Both of the men would get temporary apparel while the cleaning woman, who looked like a bag lady Hank had arrested once, washed and dried his soiled clothes.

After getting showered and donning new apparel, Jack entered the office.

Jack, Hank, and the owner thanked Will for his help. Will turned and went outside to his truck. He climbed in, turned the ignition, and headed home.

Hank, standing nearby, said, "Well, it's great not to smell myself anymore. That Fels Naptha soap really does the trick. I bet I scraped ten pounds of my skin off my body while I was in the shower."

"Yeah, now you can go home to mama and eat two pounds of spaghetti."

Hank didn't appreciate Jack's humor, but he could then see Jack's demeanor was getting serious, dead serious.

"Hank, Ken has found two men and two women so far in that black crap out there. We have a serial killer on our hands, and we have to stop him before he kills again."

Hank nodded. "Was Ken able to identify any of them?"

"No, but we can. One woman was missing an arm. I would bet we found her other arm when I led the search party last week, looking for the judge. The other woman had no head. I believe that woman must be Rachel. One man had gray hair and was clutching a handkerchief in his hand. That must have been the judge. The other man had a tattoo on his arm like Leonard had. But his tattoo was a diamond with the letters "PH." That stumps me. Who is *PH* ? We'll have to wait for our CSI team to determine that."

"And what did you find snooping around the office?"

Hank smiled. "I talked to one of the garbage truck drivers before he started his run.""Yes, he said that three days ago some guy in a black pickup towing an open trailer flipped over on Highway 11A. The traffic behind him couldn't stop and destroyed most of the items in the trailer. The state troopers contacted the dump owner to pick all of it up. He said there were tables, beds, and kid's toys but nothing of any value."

"And what else did this person have to say?"

"The driver said the past few nights he has seen that same black pickup truck enter the dump and leave five minutes later. They do allow people to bring trash into the dump free of charge. Then, just the other day, the garbage driver saw that same truck driver enter the dump at sunup. He remembered that the man's dog stuck its head outside the truck's window, and barked at him. The man in the black truck yelled at the dog, calling it Chopper. The garbage driver also said a terrible smell lingered in the air for a long time after the driver left."

"Did the driver get a look at his face?" "No, it was too dark."

"That's still okay, Hank, we are closing in on the killer and his motives.

Let's get back to our station and post our latest info on the bulletin board."

Like a couple of storm troopers, Jack and Hank marched up the steps to their station and headed toward their office. They were excited by what they had found at the Larksburg dumps. Hank had in his right hand a pile of information, that he wanted to put on the bulletin board, while Jack sported a grin that went from ear to ear. Now they believed they could put all the pieces together and the case would be solved. As they marched through the doorway, however, both came to an abrupt halt.

Standing in front of the bulletin board was Joanna, her hair pulled back in a tight ponytail and holding a long wooden ruler in her right hand. She appeared to be the perfect school marm, ready to give her bad students a sound whipping if they did not behave. Having heard the thump, of the cops' heavy boots coming down the hall, she knew this time she was going to be prepared for their arrival.

Now that she could see them standing there in their nice, clean uniforms, she dropped the ruler, stood at attention, put the index finger of her left hand under her nose sideways, and raised her right arm.

"Heil, Herr Otto und Comrade Dumbkupt."

Either Hank or Jack didn't know what "Herr Otto" or "Comrade Dumbkupt" meant, or they couldn't care less, well almost. They had the facts they thought they needed to close this case. A little more thought and investigation would do it. Soon they would have the killer in custody. The one who was committing those heinous murders, and who was making all the townspeople afraid to leave their homes or send their children to school.

As Hank stepped closer to the bulletin board, he couldn't help making a fatal comment. "You look like a schoolmaster's daughter. Where did you get that silly imitation with the finger under the nose? It's not Halloween."

That is all the ammunition Joanna needed. "My daddy, remember, he's your boss, taught me that when I was in kindergarten. His father taught him the same thing during the terrible days of World War II. Oh, I forgot you weren't even a twinkle in your father's eye back then, were you?"

Joanna picked up the ruler. "He also taught me that if the enemy gets too close, you stab him with your bayonet." Joanna made a fake lunge with the ruler. "This isn't a bayonet, but it will do. How about I run this up your rectum and make you into a vanilla Popsicle?"

Hank fired back. He recalled a World War II idiom he had once heard in a veteran's home. "Your mother wears combat boots."

"Oh, now you're a smart ass. Is your name Kilroy, by chance? The cartoon guy sticking his nose in where it didn't belong?"

By this time Jack was reclining in his seat and getting pretty tired of their tirade. He felt there were much more important matters to be settled. "Will both of you please shut up. Both of you can play soldiers later. Right now I want Hank to put all our new information on that board. I need to see it now.""And Joanna, aren't you afraid your father might show up and get us all into trouble?"

"Touchy, isn't he?" Joanna whispered in Hank's ear.

Hank laid out the pieces of information on his desk, and began sifting through them. He was having a difficult time trying to decide just where each piece should be placed on the bulletin board. Difficult logic wasn't one of his fortes.

Joanna responded to Jack's question. "My father is escorting Samantha Jurvis, our soon-to-be mayor, God help us, to the pep rally in Mayfield's town hall. Her party thinks she is a shoo-in, so they are having a big celebration before the election. It starts in the early afternoon and lasts through the night. My father, of course, is enjoying every bit of it while my mother sits at home alone.

"I did ask him why the next mayor was in this office early in the morning, and he told me it was none of my business."

Jack could feel Joanna's words. *Why are our parents married if they don't enjoy each other's company?* He wondered. "What about Samantha's husband? Where is he?"

"I guess he decided to stay home with the kids. He's not much of a public figure."

"You don't like Samantha much, do you?"

"No, I don't. I remember her from high school, and she was the weirdest person. Nobody really liked her. She would hang out with a couple of nerds for a while, and then she would hang out with a couple of bullies. She didn't seem to fit in with school life. And now she is the belle of the ball. Everyone is enraptured by her words and her looks, even my poor father. She is an evil woman, I tell you."

"Evil woman or not, I want two brief answers from you. Did you finish your newspaper assignment, and why are you here?"

Joanna moved a little closer to Jack's desk, furrowing her brow in annoyance. "Yes, I finished my assignment. The history of our glorious Mayfield and the evil founders who made it what it is will be featured in tomorrow's paper as a supplement. Be sure to read it!"

"I intend to. Now, why, I repeat, are you here?"

Joanna stepped back and pointed to the bulletin board. "You see all the information you have here? It is incomplete."

Hank stopped sorting the papers and looked back. "What do you mean its incomplete? Do you have any information you are keeping from us?"

"Yes, I do. I looked over this board when you were not around, and drew my own conclusions. You, ams, have been spending all of your time looking for the hen, while I decided to look for its nest. You know, hens do lay eggs, and I found some pretty big ones."

Jack sat up. His grin was gone. He was upset but willing to listen. "What are you telling us, Joanna?"

"At first I questioned David's story about being held captive by a sniper on duty twenty-four hours a day. I looked over some key points I received from my many sources. Then, when I thought the coast was clear, I checked out the concrete cave. I had a hard time finding it, but it was there, just as David had said it was. I climbed down into the cave, and using a rifle range graph Jake had lent me, I calculated what must have been the trajectory of the bullets that were being fired from across the Highway 11A. The graph showed me the spot where the other end of the trajectory should be.

"With a little sleuthing at our local airport, I found an aerial map taken last month of the Whiskey Creek area. There was a small trailer at the exact location I had determined from the graph. I had the hen's nest. I was sure of it."

Jack and Hank were not the happy cops who had marched in earlier. Jack spoke. "So just where this nest is you are talking about?"

"It is at the end of Clearwater Street. Remember, Samantha Jurvis lives on Clearwater Street. A winding dirt road leads back to a trailer that is partially hidden in a grove of trees. Inside I found a lot of our answers."

"You didn't break in, did you?"

Joanna nodded. "I sure did. Arrest me, but, first, let me tell you what I found. Then you can place it on your board, and put me in handcuffs."

"It probably won't be allowed in a court of law, and we probably will be hung out to dry, but we'll take it. Anything to get this killer off our streets." Jack's ego was deflated, but he forced himself to continue listening.

"There was crap all over the place. Ten times worse than the judge's place. Shell casings, fast food boxes, dog crap. You name it and it was there. On the wall was a large photo of a woman holding a three-year-old boy? I noticed a tattoo on her shoulder that read "Alfa.""

"In the living room was a wooden stand with a .30-06 rifle clamped to it. The end of the barrel was pointing through a small round hole that had been cut in the glass window. A series of cables led to a black box under the stand. On the back of the box was a red diode that kept flashing while I was there. Another cable was connected to the scope mounted on the rifle. The sights had been removed. I think the killer had the rifle sighted in on that concrete cave, and any time it detected movement, it would fire a round or two. The setup ran twenty-four hours a day. Nothing was safe near that cave. Even a rabbit would have caused the rifle to fire."

"On closer inspection, I noticed that an off switch next to the diode light had been thrown too. That is why no cops or investigators would ever be in danger. All the killer had to do when he wanted the rifle to be ready to fire, was come back to the trailer, and flip the switch on. Voila. It was ready to fire."

Joanna scrunched up her nose. "I had to get out of that place fast. The stench was overpowering, and it was getting to me."

Jack then said. "Leonard Anders said some black man named Fred Brown was fired upon trying to get near that concrete cave, and that happened many years ago."

"Yes, that could be true. But I think someone has picked up on the idea and is using it today. The CSI lab will find more answers when they, legally, enter the premises."

Hank had a retort ready. "Okay, let's say you found the killer's nest. Tell us who lived there. And why didn't you worry the killer might come back? Pretty gutsy, I'd say."

Hank looked toward his partner for support. "Right, Jack?"

"Hank is absolutely right. You were taking a big chance. We still are not sure it was only one killer. What if he had an accomplice who returned to the trailer? You would have been another dead body on our list."

"You're right."

"For heaven's sake," Jack said. "please let us in on your next adventures. Remember, you are my only sister, like it or not."

"Yes, brother, I will keep that thought in mind. But to answer Hank's question about who lives there. I found only one toothbrush in the dirty bathroom, and no indication anyone else ever was there. The killer acted alone. I am convinced of it, and I believe that guy, Alfa, is our killer."

"Was our killer! He died in a truck accident."

Joanna was stunned. "Really?" "As for who owned the place, I found no paperwork in any of the drawers. I even traced the tag on the trailer and came up empty. The ground that it sits on is part of the state's game lands. People squat there all the time until they are chased away."

"So you say Alfa was our killer. Maybe we have a ghost posing as a hit man?" Jack said, coolness leaving him.

Joanna tried to placate Jack just a little. "No, this person was a fiendish killer who took no prisoners and cuts them up for fun. You and Hank have come so close to his identity, and I have added a little more information to that board.""Sit back, brother, and relax. I'll get you a Coke. You study the board and the new facts Hank will be putting up. With that big brain of yours, I believe it's your time to close this case."

A few hours passed without any results. Each person had a different opinion on who the killer was. Hank had come to a conclusion the day before that Leonard Anders wasn't telling the truth. He had been holding Rachel hostage and trying to get more money from her father, the judge. The hateful judge must have put the word out to find Rachel, and then kill all the members of Leonard's secret club.

Joanna chose a different path of logic. She felt Leonard wasn't a capable leader. A more sinister person had to be the brains behind all this. Someone, who had enough money to bankroll the club, is allowing that person to dictate the rules and control the club's activities. But who? Since recent evidence had been uncovered showing the security cop had been selling cocaine to the college students, her guess was that an outside source was responsible for all the killings. The Red Rovers, a motorcycle gang in Larksburg, would not want anybody trying to muscle in on its drug territory.

Jack was not completely sure. Some things kept floating around in his mind. How many members were there in Leonard's club? What did the tattoos on the arms of the victims mean? Who would be the next killer's victim, if any? And why all the killings in such a short time span? The election was happening today, and the town's 175th anniversary celebration was tomorrow. As stupid as it might seem, Jack wondered if there was any connection between the celebration and the killings or the killer's identity.

Jack's cell phone pinged. He pulled it out of his shirt pocket, and saw there was a text message from Dan. "Jack, I tried to call this morning. There was no answer. But here are our latest findings. We found traces of silver paint on the left fender of that black truck. That silver paint is a special paint usedonly on select Mercedes cars. There are only two silver Mercedes registered in Mayfield and Larksburg Counties. We know our chief of police, Chuck Hankin, owns one, and the other one is owned by Samantha Jurvis. We checked out the chief's car, and there is no damage, but Samantha's car, we were told, just came out of the repair shop.

"The repairman told us only part of the grill had been damaged. He seemed a little nervous at the time. Also we found DNA all over the truck bed and on the front seat. Our initial tests show the DNA came from at least three different people. We think we will be able to match the judge's DNA to one of those samples we took. More later. Dan.

Both Hank and Joanna stared at Jack. The light bulb in Jack's mind lit up.

A broad ear-to-ear smile appeared on his face.

Anxious, Hank spoke. "What is that big shit-eatin' grin all about?"

"I think we need one more piece of evidence and we will have this case solved. Hank, move the letters from all the tattoos to one side of the board, and place them in a straight line."

Hank lifted the papers and reposted them with removable tape in one corner. When he was finished, he stepped aside so Jack and Joanna could see them.

The papers read, "LA, AL, PH."

"Hank and Joanna, Why do you think each tattoo had only two initials?" Hank spoke first. "I thought they were the initials of someone they loved. A girlfriend or boyfriend maybe."

Joanna said, "Could it be a secret code of some sort?"

Jack stared at the papers for a moment. "Hank, move the "PH" in front of the "LA."

Hank obliged. "What do we have?" Joanna spoke up. "We have PH, LA, AL?"

"We know the letters in Leonard's tattoo could be his initials, but there not. The letters in Alfa's tattoo could mean his name, but they don't. The tattoos do not contain any person's initials. I had Dan check it out, and he found no friends or relatives that had those initials."

"Hank, please take a paper and write the letters "*TH* " on it. Then place it on the board right after the letters "*AL* ." Hank obliged again. "Thanks Hank."

"Now that's just great," Joanna said "So we now have "PH, LA, AL, TH." That spells nothing in my book. Where are you going with this, Jack?"

A warm glow appeared in Jack's eyes. "If you remember Leonard told us that Edwin, or Alfa, liked to read Greek literature. Those tattoos, I tell you, contain the letters of the Greek alphabet. "*PH*"is phi, so our letter is "*P* ." "*LA* " is lambda, so our letter is "*L*", And "AL" is Alpha, so our letter is "A" They thought they were cute, trying to confuse us by adding a second letter to the tattoo. I, personally, did not think they were smart enough to do that.

"Now let's say we add the letter "T" after the "A". Do you see what that spells?"

Joanna responded at once. "Yes, I see the name Plato, a Greek philosopher."

"Yes. You got it. The secret club is called Plato. And, I might add, since there are only five letters in Plato, I bet there are only five members."

A puzzled Joanna asked. "But who are "*TH*" and "*OM*"? That is the sixty- four thousand dollar question. Are they the killer's next victims?"

Like the cavalry arriving on time to save the fort, the phone on Jack's desk rang.

"Hello, Jack Hankin speaking."

"Hello, Jack, this is Ken Nolan, the coroner." The voice caught Jack off guard. He hesitated. "Ken Nolan, the coroner from Larksburg." "Oh, yes. How are you doing?"

"Jack, the airport police brought another body into my lab today. I thought you might like to know there was a tattoo on this female's right arm. It was a diamond, like the ones on the bodies found at the dumps, but this one had the letters "*TH* " inside it. Also we are running a test on the substance we found in her stomach. We think it was a mixture of two ingredients. Whatever it was, it has destroyed all her organs."

"Thanks, Ken. That's very important news. Take care."

Jack ended the phone call, and looked directly at Joanna. "Part of your question has been answered. Hank, the coroner, has another body with a diamond on the right arm and "TH" inside it.

"Now I will give both of you my case analysis: "OM" means omega, our letter O, and the person with that tattoo, whoever it is, is the final piece to the puzzle. That person has played a very crafty and dangerous game. That person was like a silent partner who put up the money to make the club work. I would say all the members knew that person, but were afraid to say anything. Why? Because that person would use Edwin as a henchman to do the dirty work: eliminate all members before they could talk to the Cops?

"All the club members, just as Leonard told us in the hospital, had witnessed Edwin killing the security guard. When Leonard was framed for the murder and agreed to go to the concrete cave, all the members felt relieved. The fly in the ointment, however, was Rachel Morris. She loved Leonard enough to stay with him for seven long years, and when she had had enough, she was shot trying to escape. And like a row of dominos, the club members began to fall. Edwin was assigned to kill all of them at once. Like ASAP."

Joanna then said. "So you are saying Edwin, who was Alfa, killed all the club members except one, "omega".

"Yes, that is just what I am telling you. Whoever this omega is, watch out. That person thinks he has gotten rid of all his past problems and is free to roam, maybe, to kill again. I believe Omega, intentionally, ran Alfa off the road to kill him, and eliminate all evidence."

Hank spoke up. "So how are we going to find this person? Where do we look?"

"Hank and Joanna, my advice is to look for "OM" on the right arm of everybody you see, and we have to hope the person didn't have it removed. I think, though, that person is too proud to remove it. It is a symbol of control and power."

"And how are we going to check everybody's arm when everybody is wearing long sleeves and winter coats? Tell me this" Joanna said.

"I am sorry, Joanna; I don't have all the answers. Maybe wait till spring." "Yeah," said Hank. Wait till spring and hope there are no more killings?"

Joanna said, "Oh, I foresee possibly only one killing happening soon: that omega."

CHAPTER EIGHTEEN

One could believe that all the people living in Mayfield were gathered in the town hall, awaiting the arrival of their future mayor, Samantha Elizabeth Jurvis. Even though the polls had not closed, they were rejoicing and hugging each other repeatedly, knowing that the opposing candidate, present mayor, James Stigman, did not stand a chance of being reelected. The townsfolk believed the mayor had crippled the town's economy. On the other hand, Samantha Elizabeth Jurvis's popularity had soared, and now she had become the toast of their town. She had repeatedly proclaimed she had a plan to make Mayfield the thriving town it once was. She also knew it was just what the people wanted to hear.

In private as well as public she had announced wholesome new policies to tickle the peoples' ears. Mayfield's businesses were enthralled by her promises to make Mayfield grow. Everyone seemed excited and was anxiously awaiting for Samantha to arrive.

It had been a long and arduous term for James Stigman. There were a lot of people who could never forget losing their jobs and their savings during his time in office. The mayor had created a very serious job loss when he would not offer a better deal to keep the athletic shoe manufacturers and the unions of Mayfield from relocating to a new industrial park in Larksburg. In turn, local unemployment skyrocketed.

Samantha, on the other hand, had convinced the local people, including the press, that she had the answers to future growth. She accomplished this feat with emotional arguments and a lot of bravado. She even went so far as to let the cat out of the bag. She said she was in private communications with a large computer equipment corporation. When she became mayor, she said, she would offer that corporation a tax-free location in Mayfield for twenty years. In return, the corporation would erect several new buildings and employ up to three thousand people. Since unemployment was over 10 percent at this time, Samantha stated that figure would drop to 3 percent by the end of two years. She loved to raise her right arm and yell that Mayfield was going high tech. The people were ecstatic. Their minds were set. Here was a local girl, born and raised in Mayfield, who was truly concerned about her town and the people who lived there.

That had been her spiel all through the primary, and now the crowd inside the hall was eager to see Samantha make her appearance. Caterers were busy carrying trays of drinks and hors d'oeuvres throughout the hall. Beer and wine flowed like Whiskey Creek during the rainy season. The mood was very festive and was charged with reassurance and hope for the future. Posters and banners announcing Samantha Jurvis were strung on the rafters and walls. She was the one to lead the way. The entire crowd agreed, that is, except for one person.

Mayor Stigman's oldest son, Marcus, had somehow slipped past the guards at the door and moved through the crowd until he was standing directly below the stage. He had heard enough of Samantha's damn bragging and pontificating. He had come to set the record straight, not with a gun, mind you, but with a cocktail glass. It was a cocktail glass filled with a Bloody Mary, which he proudly held in his hand. He had found out Samantha had a fetish for neatness and a vile temper to match. When small things didn't go exactly her way, she would rant vehemently at a subordinate, but never did she point the finger at herself. That was strictly taboo. She believed she could do no wrong. Unfortunately, the townsfolk were never allowed to see that side of her.

Marcus knew his father was not the person to be blamed for the unemployment crises. Marcus worked as a guard at the county prison. One afternoon he had listened to an informant, a jail stoolie, who told him he had known Samantha during her college days. Then she was a big conniver and a cheat. The stoolie also said that he had been a temporary bodyguard for Samantha in her early political career, and that she had still been the same conniver and a cheat at that time. Recently, a visitor told the stoolie what she was up to. Samantha had organized a secret powwow with the shoe manufacturers and the mayor of Larksburg. At that powwow she simply stated she had proof the Larksburg mayor had committed some serious crimes, infidelity and embezzlement. The Larksburg mayor, in turn, looked stunned and embarrassed but gave no rebuttal. He was a dead duck, and he knew it.

With the aid of the athletic shoe manufacturer's finance manager, the Larksburg mayor had stolen several million dollars in stock items, and he had fondled the finance manager to boot. Samantha then decided to play her trump card. She coerced the

Larksburg mayor to make a substantial offer to the athletic shoe manufacturers to move to Larksburg, and she also applied pressure to the shoe manufacturers to move out of Mayfield. This created the unemployment situation she wanted, allowing her to brighten her pathway to being the next mayor, and, someday, the first woman president of the United States. Samantha's scheme had worked to perfection.

Marcus took a step forward and raised his glass. He knew he was in the right position to greet Samantha after she entered the hall and stood on the stage above him. It was just a matter of time. He had the patience to stand and wait.

It was pitch black outside the police station except for a few streetlights. There was no moon shining on the three people as they headed toward their cars. Jack, Hank and Joanna were finished with their arguments and theories, and were about to go home and watch the voting results on TV.

"Well, Joanna," Jack said, "I am glad you completed your newspaper assignment. I only wish Hank and I could say we have completed our assignment too. It's been a whirlwind of a case with lots of evidence and so little to show for it."

"Don't feel so bad, Jack." Joanna said. "I think you and Hank have done a superb job. I could not have done a better job myself." She smiled.

Both Jack and Hank were surprised by Joanna's comments. Had the belligerent, sarcastic woman changed her colors? Was she really sincere?

Hank stopped beside his battered sedan and looked back. "Joanna, I am sorry for anything I might have said to you that was out of line. I know you took personal risks to gather evidence and back us up. I thank you for that."

"Hank, I do appreciate that. And now I think I should tell both of you some good news."

"Good news? Are we getting a raise?"

"No, not just yet, but both of you probably wondered why my dad, your boss, didn't assign more detectives to this case."

"Yes, we have been wondering why."

"Well, he told me he wanted to see how well you two would do solving a case on your own. Just you two, nobody else, except for the CSI team when they were needed. He also wanted me to keep a sharp lookout for your safety and report to him what was going on each day. Yes, I made up the story about what he would do to us if he found us together working on this case, but keep in mind he still is a real pain in the ass at times."

Hank was not pleased. "Good news? That grumpy old bastard set us up, and you knew it all the time." Because of the shadows streaking across their faces, Joanna wasn't sure of their reaction, but she guessed they were not pleased. He shook his head. "He is always bad-mouthing you, sweetheart. Was that just a ploy too?"

"He has always been that way, and he will never change. You just have to live with it, like my mother has. And one other thing: if he had thought you were in any real danger, he would have sent the whole police force in to help you."

Jack jumped in. "And what about your newspaper? Did your boss know what you were doing?"

"No, I helped my father strictly on the QT."

Feeling numb, Jack opened the car door. "I offer my personal thanks to you too, Joanna. Maybe someday we will find our killer. The mastermind who is behind all this, Good night."

Hank entered his car and reached for the key, as Jack settled into his own car. Joanna offered her final thought.

"Rest assured, as I said before, that the police and the mayor were pleased with your efforts. Oh, and speaking of mayors, I am going down to the town hall to look around. Want to come along?"

"No, I have had enough for one day." Jack backed his car up and drove away.

"Me too," I think I am having leftover spaghetti tonight." With that, he exited the lot.

Joanna stood in silence, watching her favorite cops driving away. Then she climbed into her red sports car and sped away.

At the doors of the town hall, Joanna presented her newspaper pass to the guard, and said she was going to do a cover story on Samantha. Meandering her way through the noisy crowd, she was consistently on the lookout for newsworthy items to print in the newspaper.

Joanna had to smile. Several people were staring at her. She remembered her newspaper boss telling her more and more people were reading her columns. Newspaper sales were at an all-time high. Here in the town hall she could see it was really true. These people were acknowledging who she was.

Joanna had a thought. *I bet my story on the corruption in our courts has awakened the town.*

The guards opened the front doors wide, and a blast of music flowed into the hall. Because there were tall men standing in front of her, Joanna had to jump up a few times to get a glimpse of the world-renowned Mayfield High School band. Wearing stars and stripes uniforms, they began to march into the town hall and head for the stage. About a hundred band members filed past Joanna. They were playing "Green Grass of Summer." Joanna could hear a bystander say to his wife that song was Samantha's favorite. Joanna made a mental note of that.

At the tail end of the band, a man and a woman dressed to the nines were smiling and waving to the crowd as they entered and walked directly toward the stage. Their two small children were trying to stay close to their parents. Joanna could see the children were frightened, probably because of all the hoopla going on. One of the security guards talked briefly with them and led them away to the game room downstairs.

The marching band continued to the back of the hall while Samantha and her husband climbed the few steps leading up to the stage. The people clapped and yelled as they grouped around the stage. Samantha and her husband continued to smile and wave.

It was a blissful scene.

The music ended as Samantha stepped up to the microphone and addressed the crowd. "Ladies and gentlemen, and all the children as well. The long march to the mayor's office is about over. I will be your new leader in a few minutes, and I will try to be a good one for all of you out there."

Samantha raised Carl's arm in victory. "My husband, Carl, has been gracious enough to be with me here tonight. His work is at home, and it keeps him so busy he has to sleep during the day. We do not see each other that often, but that doesn't matter. I love him so much."

The crowd clapped, showing their approval.

A slightly embarrassed Carl, sporting a little smile, moved closer to Samantha and gave her a kiss on the cheek. He turned away and exited the stage. The crowd responded by clapping harder.

Samantha didn't bother to watch him leave but offered a thought to the crowd. "Ladies, if you have a great and wonderful husband or boyfriend, do not let him go." She leaned into the microphone." "Thanks, Carl, for coming with me tonight."

Marcus saw his opportunity. With a mighty toss, he aimed his glass at Samantha. The glass made an arc in flight and hit Samantha on the right shoulder. She winced as the red liquid of the Bloody Mary flowed down her white dress. The celery stalk slid down and lodged itself in her dress pocket.

Being a stickler for neatness, Samantha looked down at Marcus and let out a terrible scream. "You son-of-a-bitch. You bastard. You ruined my party. I am going to put your ass in a sling, just like I did to your father. This town belongs to the Jurvises. It was founded and owned by the Jurvises' until your weasel father got elected. I am here to take it back for the Jurvises where it rightly belongs."

Samantha looked around the hall. The crowd was quiet. They were stunned.

"Where's a security guard when you need one? Get this shithead out of my sight now."

The crowd stood motionless as two security guards pushed through. They grabbed Marcus and started to escort him away. A hush settled over the crowd. As Marcus was being hauled away, he looked back. "You vampire! You fraud!" "You suck the life out of this town and do not care about who you hurt. My father, James Stigman, is innocent."

Samantha gained her composure quickly and acted though nothing had happened. "Everybody, please forgive me. Would someone in the audience please help me to the ladies' room? I need to change my clothing before the rest of our celebration starts." Samantha asked her personal assistant to pick a new outfit from her limo as Joanna Hankin stepped up on the stage.

"Thank you for coming forward to help me." "I am Joanna Hankin. I will assist you."

"I know who you are. I have read your newspaper column each day. I remember our times growing up in this wonderful town?"

"Yes, I do too."

Samantha grabbed the hem of her gown and handed it to Joanna. "Take this so I don't fall, and follow me to the ladies' room."

Joanna cringed at her words. *Am I your slave?* she thought. She grabbed the hem of the gown and followed Samantha down the steps and to the ladies room. The people began to loosen up, as the caterers handed out more drinks.

As Samantha entered the ladies room, she was livid once again. "How could that damn bastard ruin my two thousand-dollar dress?"

Joanna dropped the hem and looked Samantha in the eye. "The police have that guy in custody now, and he will have to pay for your dress. Cheer up! You're the new mayor of Mayfield."

Samantha would have no part of what Joanna was saying. "An eye for an eye" was her secret motto. To Hell with the law, she would have her friends make this guy squeal like a pig.

"Here, let me help you." Joanna said as she reached to unbutton Samantha's shoulder straps.

"Don't worry about the shoulder straps. Just pull this damn dirty thing off me. I'll just put the cost of the gown on Mayfield's budget."

Samantha's assistant brought a new gown exactly like the one Samantha had been wearing, into the ladies room, and laid it on the counter next to the sink. Then she left without saying a word.

Joanna tried in vain to break the knots that connected the shoulder strap. Finally, she had to tear each strap. Joanna watched Samantha as the gown slowly slid down her lithe body. This soon-to-be mayor was a beautiful, shapely woman. Even after having two children, Samantha still had the shape of a beauty queen.

The gown stopped at Samantha's breast while Joanna removed the left arm from the sleeve. Then she moved to the other side and began to remove the right arm. As the smooth, silky skin of Samantha's right arm became apparent, Joanna stopped and stared at a tattoo. It was a diamond with legs and the letters "OM" inside it.

"What are you staring at, Joanna? Yes, I know all about you and those stupid editorials you have been writing in the newspaper. And yes, that is a tattoo I received years ago while I was in college."

Joanna was stunned. She took a step backwards. "So you are Omega!

You're the mastermind behind all the killings we have had in Mayfield." "Yes, if you must know. I am not afraid to tell the public. I bankrolled a secret club to get even for the shit your school and town had thrown at me. And don't think you are going to get away. My new henchman is right outside."

Samantha let the gown fall to the tile floor and stepped out of it. She bent over and removed a small pistol that was strapped to her calf. She stood up and pointed the pistol at a stunned Joanna. "Just like Ma Barker, I always carry a weapon for safety. This little pistol will put a nice hole in your heart. And it's unmarked, so I'll tell the police it was yours. I wrestled with you, and the pistol went off. The crowd of shitheads out there in the town hall will believe me. They're so damn gullible."

"You had to destroy your club to protect yourself, and you had Alfa shut their mouths for good."

"That stooge. I made him think I cared for him. He was too easy. He disgusted me."

Joanna shook her head. "Prison isn't good enough for you."

"Quit your shit. Any last words, Miss Joanna Selden, the great newspaper reporter?"

Bam! Bam The sounds of an altercation made Joanna and Samantha turn their attention to the door. Then there was silence.

Just like Mel Gibson and Danny Glover in "Lethal Weapon", Jack and Hank burst through the door, aiming their pistols at a partially naked Samantha. "Drop the pistol now, or we will shoot!" said Jack.

A hardheaded Samantha lowered her pistol a little, and stepped backwards until her back was against the stall door. In a flash, she fired at Joanna and pushed backwards into the stall. She bolted the door and fired several shots through the crack between the door and door mounting. One bullet hit Jack in the hip. As he fell to the floor, he fired four rounds, which punctured the stall door.

Hank held his fire because he could hear something fall to the floor. He went over to the stall and slowly opened the door. He could see Samantha was lying against the toilet bowl. She was not moving. He lifted the cell phone from his shirt pocket, and called 911. After a short conversation with the dispatcher, he approached Jack to see how he was doing.

Jack winced from the pain. "I'm okay. Well, sorta. Please check on my sister."

Hank walked over the far wall. Joanna was clutching her left arm, and blood was dripping through her fingers. "I called," he said, "and a medical team will be here in a minute. Can I do anything for you?"

"No, I can wait for medical help."

Hank and Joanna walked back to Jack, who was still lying on the floor. Jack readjusted his body and looked up. "Are you okay, sis?"

"Yes I am, except for a bullet wound in my arm. That damn pistol Samantha used missed my heart by inches. She should have had it sighted in. But now that I think about it, it's a good thing she didn't. Otherwise, both of you would have no one to kick your asses." Joanna could see Jack was trying to smile, but the pain was stopping him. "How did you know I was here?"

Hank had to field this question. "After we left you at the police station, both of us talked it over on our cell phones, and decided we should be there in the town hall with you. As for knowing what was going on in the ladies' room, we heard everything, and so did the crowd outside. You see, there is a loudspeaker mounted on the wall in the town hall. A guard said the people wanted to know how Samantha was. All we had to do was turn the switch on."

"Well, you solved the case, Hank and Jack." "No, we did. You, Joanna, are part of our team."

Two hours later, the voting results were officially announced. Samantha Jurvis had won by an overwhelming margin. No one cared.